A Thanksgiving Blessing

A Thanksgiving Blessing

Rebecca March

Inscript

Inscript

Published by Inscript Books
a division of Dove Christian Publishers
P.O. Box 611
Bladensburg, MD 20710-0611
www.inscriptpublishing.com

Inscript and the portrayal of a pen with script are trademarks of Dove Christian Publishers.

Book Design by Mark Yearnings

ISBN: 978-1-7359529-4-9

This book is, first and foremost, dedicated to My Heavenly Father, who gave me the idea to write this book and gave me the passion to write years ago.

To my family and friends who have read countless book drafts and encouraged me to keep writing no matter what.

But most importantly, to all the military member's significant others, spouses, and family members who have gone through the unthinkable. This book is in honor of those who have made the ultimate sacrifice for this country.

Chapter One

Lacy looked out her office window and thought to herself about how Thanksgiving was just around the corner. Lacy valued her family and, despite living far away from them, she rarely missed the holidays with them. She had one more event standing in her way before she would go on the plane to head home. For the last five years, Lacy has been an event planner since she moved from home near DC to a medium-sized suburban town in Kansas. She loved being the one who could bring joy to others through her decorations and creative ideas. Her business blossomed throughout the years, and she had many recurring clients whom she helped prepare for their special events. She would do all different kinds of events, from birthday parties to fourth of July celebrations, weddings, and more. Her favorite kinds of events were decorating for weddings and helping men with marriage proposal ideas.

Actually, the current event she worked on was a proposal. The boyfriend wanted to make everything extra special to propose to his girlfriend. He had an idea in his head, but he needed Lacy to help the idea come to life. The majority of her clients just needed the extra help but had a vision of how they wanted the event to look. They worked hard on sketches and finding everything to make his dream become a reality. The day finally arrived for them to set up and execute the plan. Then the next day, she would be on her way back home to Virginia, to a suburb about 30 minutes away from D.C.

After daydreaming for a few minutes, Lacy returned to reality and made a phone call to her client, Grant, who finally decided to ask his girlfriend to marry him after three years with her. Grant worked as a construction worker to help build houses in the community, and he absolutely loved his work. He had brown hair with a beard that filled up half of his face, and he was built with muscles from all the heavy work he did as a construction worker. His girlfriend, Angela, petite at 5'4" with strawberry blonde hair, met him when he was on the job site. Angela had come one day with her friend, whom the house was for, when she first met Grant. She was smitten from the start, but she tried not to make it too obvious. Grant did not say much the first time except for a simple hello because he was also smitten. She came back a few more times, and after the third time, Grant gained the courage to ask Angela on a date. It was now three years later, and he could not wait to make her his wife.

Lacy called Grant on her phone. "Hey Grant, this is Lacy. It is the big day! Are you ready?"

"Yes! I am so excited! I cannot believe that today is

the day!" Grant said with enthusiasm.

"So, what time would be a good time for me to set up everything?" Lacy inquired.

"Maybe like 2. I can always come and help. I know you said to just let me relax before the big evening, but I am here to help if you need it."

"I appreciate you wanting to help, but I want to make it a surprise for both of you."

"Okay! Then I'll see you later."

Once Lacy got off the phone, she gathered all her decorations and other items that she would need for the event and put them in the back of her car. It was already 1 pm, and the place was about 45 minutes away, so she needed to leave as soon as possible if she wanted to get there with time to spare. After coming back inside, Lacy grabbed her keys and her purse before heading back out the door. She turned the key in the ignition, and it wouldn't start.

This is interesting and horrible timing, she thought.

She tried again and, thankfully, the second time the car started. Her car was relatively new, so she was confused about why it was having trouble starting. She did not have time to think about it, and after a little while, she completely forgot about it.

On the road, cars honked, trying to get places as quickly as they could. Traffic spanned for miles and miles. She later found out the traffic was from an accident a few miles up the road. Lacy, like everyone else, did not enjoy traffic. Still, she would try to enjoy the moment by cranking up the music on the radio to pass the time. It also helped her to stay in a positive mood despite the circumstances.

Lacy ended up getting to the event place a little after 2:30 pm. She stepped out of her car and headed into the church where the proposal would take place. The church was a small white building with a few stained-glass windows. As she stepped into the church, it took her back to a memory from a few years ago. She quickly kicked the memory out of her mind because she did not want to think about it. She needed to stay on task. She walked into the small gym in the church and met up with the ladies who would help make the dinner for the couple.

"Sorry, ladies, I'm late. I ran into a little bit of traffic."

"It's okay," one of the ladies said. "We just got here ourselves. Shall we help you get the decorations out of your car?"

"Absolutely!"

Lacy and the ladies went out to her car and grabbed as much as they could in one trip. Lacy went back a few more times to bring everything into the church. The ladies made their way to the kitchen to prepare the food. Once every box was placed in the gym, Lacy closed her eyes to envision one last time how she would transform the place. She had her plans sketched out, but it always helped to close her eyes to really see how each piece would fit.

The ladies came back to the gym to check if they could help with anything else.

"Sorry to interrupt," one of them said. "We are going to start on dinner unless you need help with decorating."

"I think that I am good right now. I will let you know later if I need any help," Lacy replied.

Lacy sometimes would ask for help from others, but usually, first, she tried to do things on her own. She gathered up the LED lights and started stringing them around the room. She placed them so that the lights were hanging down from the ceiling to look like a place in a fairytale. The lights flickered and reflected off the windows to make it even more magical. Then, on the ground, she placed fake leaves to make it a fall wonderland. The fake leaves consisted of three different colors: neon red, yellow, the color of the sun, and orange that resembled the color of a traffic cone. Grant wanted the place to look like an autumn wonderland since his girlfriend Angela loved the fall season more than any other. When Lacy finished, it looked just like that. She moved a small two-person table from the hallway and carried it into the gym. She put a white and orange tablecloth on the small table and then decorated the table with small little leaves and pumpkin confetti. The next time she checked her phone for the time, it was three hours later, and she only had one thing left to do. She reached in the bottom of the last box for the mason jar candles that would give the finishing touch of the feeling of fall. After she put it on the table, she stepped back to see the whole panorama of the room. Lacy double-checked one last time that everything looked perfect. She glanced around the room, took a few pictures that she could refer to for other events, and then headed to her car to store all the empty boxes. As she packed up, Grant arrived at the church. He was dressed in a nice fall sweater and khaki pants.

His hands shook nervously as he began to speak.

"Everything done?" You could hear the anxiety in his voice.

"Yes, I just finished."

"Good because she should be arriving any minute now. Can I see the finished product?"

"Yes, go in there and make sure that everything is up to your standard."

He walked into the church and through the hallway to the gym. As he walked in, his eyes lit up and widened. He was speechless for a few minutes.

"This is literally everything and more. I can't believe how this turned out. Wow."

"Thank you. I just took your dream and made it happen."

"You did more than that."

"Thank you. It was nothing."

"No, it was not. It is so amazing. I couldn't have asked for it to be anything more."

Grant then headed to the bathroom to freshen up one last time before his girlfriend arrived. He made sure to bring some mouthwash and a comb just in case the ride over messed up his hair. He swigged a cap of cinnamon mouthwash back and forth in his mouth. After rinsing until it seemed as if the mouthwash was about to burn the top of his mouth, he spit it out. With a sigh of fresh breath, he checked that nothing was left in his teeth. Then he combed a small piece of hair that had flown up on the ride over.

While he got ready, Lacy headed to the kitchen to ensure that everything was ready and prepared for dinner. "Hello, ladies. I hope all is well. It smells amazing. I just wanted to let you know Grant is here, and Angela is on her way. Are you almost finished up?"

One of the ladies answered on behalf of the others. "Yes, we just have the bread in the oven finishing up, and then everything will be ready!"

"Thank you so much for your help!"

"No, thank you. We looked in the gym, and it doesn't look anything like it did before. You really have a way with making your sketches come alive."

"Thank you so much. I just love being creative and the smile on someone's face when they see the finished product."

She thanked the women one last time and then walked down the hallway to check on Grant one last time. Grant came out of the bathroom and let everyone know that Angela had just given him an update that she was five minutes away. Lacy's work was done, and she needed to leave before Angela got there. She wished Grant the best of luck and then got in her car to drive away. She wished she could stay to see the proposal, but sometimes it did not work that way. Lacy left just as Angela pulled into a parking spot. In most cases, she would go later that night or the next day to clean up the place, but the church said that it would be fine to leave up the decorations for the church Thanksgiving dinner. They told Lacy that she could take them down when she got back to Kansas after the holiday.

This time the roads were clear, and she had no problem with traffic. She put her car on cruise control and had the whole road to herself for most of her drive home. Before long, she got back into her apartment. She pulled into a spot outside of her apartment and ran inside.

Time flew by. It was 7 pm, and her flight to leave to go home only was 10 hours away. She still needed to pack a few more things in her suitcase. The majority she had packed the day before, but there were a few more things in the laundry that still needed to dry before she could pack them up. She packed nice clothes for Thanksgiving along with workout and lounge clothes for the remainder of her stay. Once she was home, she did not plan on going anywhere fancy, so she knew she would be okay with just a few outfits. Also, it would not be a huge deal if she did forget something since she still had a little stash of clothes at home.

As she headed back to the kitchen, her stomach growled, telling her to eat. Lacy realized at that moment that she had not eaten anything all day. She looked in her refrigerator, realizing that there was only a jar of tomato sauce and some cheese. Then she looked in her pantry and found some pasta, so she immediately decided to make a big bowl of pasta. She wanted to have a big dinner so that she did not have to eat anything other than a snack or two until she got to DC. The flight would only be about 4 hours, so she would arrive in DC around 9 in the morning.

She made her big bowl of pasta, sprinkled a hint of Parmesan on the top, and turned on the TV to see if any movie or show was on. There was nothing really interesting on, so she just turned to the news to update herself on what was going on in the world. Sometimes Lacy would forget to check the news because she worked hard to prepare for events and did not take the time. She also did not want to watch the news all day because it could be depressing, and sometimes, she felt like avoiding it. Before long, she fell asleep on the couch, only to wake up at 3 am.

"Wow, I'm glad that I woke up now. I could have missed my flight," Lacy said out loud.

She grabbed her suitcase and her carry-on bag and headed out the door. She got into her car and headed to the local airport, about an hour away. Luckily, it was Saturday morning, and she was able to drive without running into any traffic. Cars on the roads were scarce, with only two or three the whole way to the airport. She arrived at the airport at 4 am with an hour of extra time before boarding. She checked in her suitcase and then sat at the gate. She still had some time to spare, so she took a book out of her carry-on and began reading. She texted her family on the family group chat about her departure, along with a GIF of an airplane taking off. Before long, they called her flight number, and it was time to board the plane. Once she got to her seat in 16B, she sat down, put her bag on her lap, and continued reading her book. The book transported her into another world of fantasy and romance. All the noises around her faded as she engrossed herself in the story. She did not even recognize it when someone sat next to her before the flight took off. She came back to reality when the flight attendant announced, "Please return to your seats for landing."

Four hours flew by in an instant, and the plane landed at the DC airport. She waved to the person sitting next to her as he walked out to exit the plane, hoping that he did not think she was rude for not saying anything the whole flight. Lacy went to the baggage claim to retrieve her suitcase. As she was waiting for it to come on the conveyor belt, she looked around and saw men and women in uniform greeting their families.

She could not help but smile, seeing them hugging each other after such a long time apart. She saw one couple run to each other and meet each other halfway. The man in uniform took his wife in his arms and gave her a passionate kiss that seemed minutes long. After such a long time apart, no wonder the kiss would last more than a minute. They had so many months to make up for. Then Lacy watched as they walked away, holding on to each other as if life depended on it.

She saw another woman in uniform that saw her kids and immediately dropped her bags to run to them. Her kids yelled "Mommy" over and over again until their mom reached them. Her husband slowly moved towards her after the kids got a few minutes of alone time with her. Lacy loved these greetings. It was one of the reasons she went into event planning in the first place. There was just something about love that made her smile, and she could not help but watch to see the unfolding of each story. Some people might call it creepy to people-watch, but couples like these inspired her sketches.

After about five more minutes, her suitcase arrived, and she grabbed it. She could not miss it as it went along the conveyor belt because it was a nice bright blue solid color with a football travel tag attached to the handle. Then she went outside to get a cab that would take her home. Her family lived just outside of DC, and it would only be a 30-minute drive, maybe a little bit more with the holiday traffic. It did not take long for a cab to come. She got into the cab and told the cab driver the address. The cab driver put it in his GPS, and after a few moments of silence, he began talking.

"Are you going home for the Thanksgiving holiday?"

"Yes."

"Where are you coming from?"

"I'm coming from Kansas, so it was not too bad of a flight. Are you going to have to work on Thanksgiving, or are you doing something, too?"

"Luckily, I am able to get off this year, and I will be spending it with my family."

"That is great!"

The cab driver quickly changed the subject. "Do you mind if I put some Christmas music on? I know that it is before Thanksgiving, but I start listening to it after Halloween."

"I'm the same way. Go for it."

One Christmas song played, and they sat in silence before both of them started singing to the music at the top of their lungs. She no longer felt that she was in the car with a stranger but with a friend. They continued singing all the way to her house. Before long, the cab arrived in front of her parent's house. She knew that everyone would be off to work and that she would be arriving at an empty house. She gave the cab driver money for the trip, wished him a great Thanksgiving and Merry Christmas, and then walked up to the front door.

She grabbed the front door key out of her pocket and turned it in the lock. It was her first time coming home without anyone else there. As she walked through the house, it felt so empty and cold. The good and bad memories flooded back through her mind. She could not wait until it was filled up with her family again and more good memories could consume the bad ones. The house felt bigger than she remembered as she walked upstairs to her old room. It looked almost identical to the last time, with the same family pictures hanging on the wall and the furniture in the same place. The only thing that looked out of place was the pile of boxes in the living room. As she approached the room, she reminded herself that the boxes must contain some of the Christmas decorations her mom started to get from the basement.

Then she remembered that she needed to let her family know she had arrived home safely. She texted her family that she had made it back safe and sound. For the time being, her mom, dad, and Hannah, her younger sister who was away at college, lived at the house. Even for them, it felt like a big house, especially with Lacy gone the last five years. Her mom texted her back a few minutes later, which soon turned into a short phone call. Her phone rang, and the caller ID read *Mom.*

"Hey, Sweetie. I know that you just got back, but if you want to decorate and clean up the house after you've rested, that would be a great help."

"How did I know that you would say that? I will rest for a little bit and get to work. Are all the decorations out in the boxes?

"Yes, they are in the boxes. Just do some cleaning and get our guest room ready. You can decorate the guest room and indoors with Christmas decorations, but then we will do the rest together after Thanksgiving."

"Okay, Mom, see you later."

Lacy went up the stairs once more to take her suitcase to her old room, and then she came downstairs to get something out of the fridge for breakfast. She found an orange and some leftover French toast to warm up to eat. She sat down on the couch and ate while watching a baking show on TV. Then after an hour, with the strength she mustered, she vacuumed and dusted the house. It was two hours later when she finished cleaning. She took some of the decorations from the box and began hanging them around the room and upstairs. The house looked like Christmas, and now she needed a much-deserved nap.

Chapter Two

She was down for the count for about two more hours when she woke up to a knock at the door. She froze in place on the couch. She tried to get up, but it was like her muscles and every bone in her body could not move. She sat paralyzed for a moment. The memory of five years ago, the day before Thanksgiving, came vividly back to her mind.

~ Five Years Ago ~

It was the day she was supposed to see James, her fiancé, after his deployment to Afghanistan. She anxiously waited. She received no communication that he was back in the States. She started to worry that he would not make it home in time. She was home after a long day of working on an event, and in her mind, she cycled through different worse-case scenarios. She tried with all her might to control her thoughts, but something in her gut told her that something was wrong. There was a knock on the door. She froze, knowing that most people rang the doorbell when they visited her. Her heart dropped, realizing that if she opened the door, her worst nightmare would come true. When she composed herself, she opened the door, and her worst nightmare stood right in front of her. There were two officers dressed in uniform, and they asked to come in. Usually, the officers would only visit family members to tell them the information, but since her fiancé, James, no longer had living parents, he chose Lacy to be contacted instead.

"Lacy. We are sorry to inform you that your fiancé was killed in action."

That is all Lacy heard before she felt the ground moving below her. She wanted to cry, but she couldn't. All she could say to the men was, "Thank you for letting me know," and then walked them out. Things were never the same after that.

~

*L*acy came back to reality and started to feel strength return to her body as she pushed off the couch to stand on her feet and walk to the door. She opened the door to a stranger, a very fine-looking man in his Navy dress blues with brown hair and piercing green eyes. As he looked at her for the second time, she stood paralyzed, but this time for another reason. The man smiled and said something to her, but all she could think of was that moment when she and her fiancé met for the first time. The mystery man in uniform looked like almost a spitting image of her former fiancé except for minor details. For a split second, she wondered if she was dreaming or if the last five years she believed a lie. She soon snapped out of it and finally acknowledged the man in front of her.

"I'm sorry. I'm Lacy Winters. Who are you?"

"Hi, I'm Nathan Thompson. Your mom invited me to come to your house for Thanksgiving since I couldn't go home to my family."

"Oh, she didn't mention that to me. Do you mind me asking how old you are?" It was a random question to ask a stranger and maybe not the most appropriate one after just meeting him. Still, she let her curiosity get the better of her.

"Oh, then I am sorry. I arrived a little early. And yes, I'm 28. Mom told me never to ask a woman's age, but since you asked...."

"I'm 26! Well, that makes sense then that she wanted me to clean the house and the guest room," Lacy said as she rolled her eyes and wondered why her mom did not say anything.

"I know we just met, but you seem distant. Are you okay?"

Lacy, not knowing Nathan, replied simply, "Yes, I am doing fine."

"Okay." Nathan did not believe it, but he would not push any further.

"I'm sorry. Where are my manners? Come in, and I can show you a tour of the house and let you settle in."

Nathan walked into the house, and he immediately

felt at home. The decorations reminded him of the decorations back at his childhood home. He knew that even though he could not go home, he would have a good time this Thanksgiving.

Last year, Lacy's mom started to look for an opportunity to have a service member over for Thanksgiving. She knew it would be hard for Lacy to see someone in uniform again, but she also knew that it might lead to healing for her. At the beginning of the year, Lacy's mom contacted the local base to see if any service members needed a place to stay for Thanksgiving. In the beginning, the base did not have anyone who signed up for a place to stay for Thanksgiving; however, but a few months later, she got a phone call that a navy corpsman was looking for a family to spend Thanksgiving with since he could not go home due to training.

When he first saw Lacy as she opened the door, he was taken aback by her beauty. Her light blonde hair in a ponytail and baby blue eyes caught his eye from the moment she looked up. Something about her seemed familiar. He never saw someone so broken and beautiful. It made him even more intrigued about her.

"Nathan..."

"I'm sorry, I was just taking in all the beauty that this house has to offer. Did you say something?"

"I just said would you like to see your room? It seems that we are both in our own world today." "Oh yeah, just thinking about something. Yes, and then I will freshen up and come back downstairs for the rest of the tour."

"Okay, take your time."

Lacy headed back downstairs to prepare some hot chocolate for her and her guest. She liked to make the hot chocolate from scratch, so she got a pot out and began warming up the water. Nathan smelled chocolate and wondered what was happening in the kitchen. He traveled down the stairs to see Lacy making something in the kitchen. She was barefoot now and so focused that she did not hear him come in. Before he said something, he stared at her as she moved around the kitchen so swiftly.

"That smells amazing."

Lacy jumped. "Oh, sorry, I didn't notice you had come back down. Would you like some hot chocolate? I just made it."

"Yes, that would be nice."

He took a sip, and his eyes opened with excitement. He never tasted hot chocolate so good. "How did you make this? It's amazing! I've never tasted hot chocolate this good before, and that is saying something. Don't tell my mother."

"Sorry, it's a secret."

"Okay, well then, I guess I'm just going to have to try to get that secret out of you."

For a second, she felt comfortable with this practical stranger but then realized that she was a little flirty and once again put her guard back up. She was not ready for anything serious. When her fiancé died, she told herself there was no way that she would date someone in the military, let alone really ever fall in love with someone again. She made a promise to herself to work hard and leave no time for love, and she planned to keep it.

Nathan interrupted her thoughts. "I don't mean to pry or make you feel uncomfortable, but I can see that something is up, and I'm a good listener if you want to talk."

"Thanks, but I'm not ready for that."

"Okay..." Nathan said he would not push her to share, but without thinking, he did it again.

They sat in silence, sipping the hot chocolate when her ringing phone broke the silence.

Lacy got up and took her phone to the next room. "Hello, who is this?"

"It's David. I just wanted to check on you and see how you are doing."

"I'm doing okay. You know today of all days is the hardest. How are you doing?"

"I've actually met someone, which doesn't make it any easier, but she is really great at listening and helps me every day to get through the pain of losing him."

"That's great. Thank you for calling, but once my family gets home, I think I'll be better. It doesn't get any easier, but I think each year I can slowly enjoy the time more."

David was one of James' friends whom he had known since high school. They remained friends until his death. Actually, he and David went to Navy boot camp together and went on all their deployments together. After James' death, David retired from the Navy, became a high school PE teacher, and absolutely loved it. He also got to coach football as a bonus, which made him happy to get up for school every morning. Lacy and David kept in contact with each other and, even after her leaving for Kansas, they talked to each other to help cope with the pain of their loss. They both lost someone that mattered deeply to them, and confiding in each other helped them slowly heal. For a time, some friends thought that David and Lacy would end up getting into a relationship, but for the two of them, the relationship never formed, and they both knew it never would.

She hung up the phone, only to be immediately interrupted again by the doorbell. In the meantime, Nathan stayed in the family room sipping his hot chocolate, and, for the second time that afternoon, he traveled off to a new place in his mind until the doorbell brought him back to reality. He was curious why all these people were calling and visiting Lacy, so he slowly tiptoed to the kitchen to see what was going on. He was not trying to be nosy, just concerned and curious.

Meanwhile, Lacy opened the door to see Tanner, another of James' friends, standing right in front of her. Tanner was James' other best friend from high school.

Before James went to Afghanistan, he asked him to watch over her if anything happened to him. Nathan thought she might let him in, but he stood outside on the front porch for over fifteen minutes. Nathan did not hear the whole conversation but only little pockets of it.

"How are you doing?" Tanner's voice traveled from the front door to the kitchen.

"You know, just trying to get through the next few days," Lacy replied.

"You know, I don't want to bring it up, but I need to. He would want you to be happy and find someone. You don't have to do this alone. He even told me to tell you that."

"I know we had that conversation, and he told me, too. It's not as easy as it sounds, though."

He heard mumbles for the rest of the conversation. Nathan was even more curious after hearing the conversation. He did not want to overstep, but he also loved to listen and just help people. He thought he was being sneaky, but Lacy turned around to see him standing in the kitchen.

"So, you've been listening."

"Yeah. I'm sorry, but I couldn't help it. You intrigued me, and I was curious."

"Well, I'm sure it will come up with my family too, so I guess you should hear it from me first." Lacy explained the whole story to Nathan, and slowly, tears dripped down her face. They kept on flowing, and she continued wiping them away. Nathan grabbed a tissue from the table and handed it to her.

Lacy took it before apologizing and leaving the room. "I'm sorry. Give me a moment."

She headed to the bathroom to blow her nose and cry some more. The tears continued to come like a waterfall that never wanted to stop flowing down. She grabbed a few more tissues and blew her nose over and over again until it became red. Ten minutes later, she came back to see Nathan, looking at her how she remembered James looked at her when they first met long ago.

"Sorry. I usually don't get emotional like that."

"You don't have to apologize, and I'm sorry for your loss."

"I'm sorry. It's just the knock on the door always brings me back to five years ago. I guess I should put something on the door that says 'do not knock, ring the bell' so I can avoid it from happening. Honestly, I don't know if I will ever be able to hear a knock on the door and not have a flashback to that night."

"Well, if it makes you feel any better, after my first deployment, I struggled with having some reoccurring dreams of one of the days we went out on a mission. It replayed in my mind every time I closed my eyes. I talked to someone about it when I got back, and luckily, I was able to continue being a corpsman for the Marines, and I haven't had the dream since. However, I wonder if something like what happened would retrigger it. I cannot fully understand, but I'm saying I know how it feels to be haunted by something."

"Yeah, out of everyone, I can never understand what you have been through...but I can see how you would understand that. I wouldn't usually tell a total stranger this, but there is something about you that is making me open up easier than usual. I've done the talking and the therapy, and it helped, but it didn't take away the pain or the flashbacks. I feel that I am doing better, and the only thing that brings me back is hearing someone knock. Isn't it crazy how one little noise can do so much to someone?"

Nathan and Lacy continued to talk for a little longer about the different difficult situations they went through. The connection between their situations made them immediately open up to each other and skip the small talk.

Lacy shared how, after her fiancé James died, she needed to get away, and that was why she moved to Kansas. "Yeah, I could no longer deal with staying in the place that it happened. So, I got an offer to work in Kansas, and I took it. Then over time, I ended up leaving that company and starting my own business. I did not want to return after that Thanksgiving, but I love my family so much that I did every year since, despite how much pain it continues to bring. Finally, after five years, I know that it will always be difficult, but each year it becomes a little bit easier to come back to the house where it happened."

"I cannot imagine how much that would be painful. My family is very important to me too. However, it was not always the case. I joined the Navy to work as a medic to get away from what was going on in my life at the time. I needed a change, and going into the Navy was me running away from the situation at home. It might have been a rash decision, but in the long run, it was the best decision I would ever make."

"So, do you work in the Navy or the Marines? I'm confused since you said you were a corpsman for the Marines, but you've also said you work for the Navy, and you are in a Navy uniform right now?"

"Yeah, it can be a little confusing. I am officially in the Navy but working as a green side corpsman, which means that I am mainly working along with Marines the majority of the time on deployment and training with them as well."

"Oh, okay. If you don't mind me asking… what situation led you to join and be a corpsman? I know that we barely know each other, but I am a good listener too if you want to talk."

"Actually, I'm pretty much an open book. I made some bad choices in high school, nothing extreme, but as you can imagine, my dad was very disappointed in me. We never got along, and I was tired of the tension in the household. I learned about the Navy one day at high school and then did research on how I could help with a medical aspect of the Navy. I came across information about a corpsman for the Marines, and ever since then, I fell in love with the idea. It was my mission from then on. I told my parents, and they did not support it at first, but eventually, over time, they grew to respect my decision. I left the day after high school graduation for boot camp. Before I left, my dad said that he was proud of me, and that was the turn in our relationship. Being in the military changed my life in so many ways, the most important saving my relationship with my father. I will forever be grateful for that."

"So, you've been a corpsman for ten years now?"

"Well, first in the Navy and then moved on to being a corpsman for the Marines after two years. I've never thought of staying in service for life, and I always wanted to eventually do something else."

"My fiancé was the opposite. He told me from the beginning that he was planning to be in the Navy for life. I knew it was going to be hard, but I had pretty much already fallen in love with him by then to change my mind."

"I know many guys who are the same way, but I have thought about it a lot, and I want to do something different and be around for my family for the future. I'm not saying those who stay in for life aren't around, but I just want to do something and have more time to spend with my family."

"It seems like you have really thought about it. So, after your next deployment, are you going to retire or switch to the reserves? I'm sure your family will be happy to have you around more."

She could not believe that she was a little bit jealous of his family. Lacy misunderstood and thought that when he said *family*, he meant that he had a wife and children of his own. The thought went into her mind, and she stopped it before she could think about it any further. It did not matter if he had a family of his own or not because she was not interested... or at least that is what she kept telling herself.

"No, I am going to be a corpsman for a few more years and then finally retire. I have not met anyone special enough to settle down with yet, so I figure I could be in for a few more years, and then it will be time to settle down and start a family." Nathan wanted to clarify any thoughts she might have and let her know that he was available in case she wondered or cared.

The conversation would have gone on for hours, but someone walked in the front door.

"Hello, Lacy, you home?" Lacy's mom's voice was heard as she walked into the house. "Yes, Mom, we are in here."

"We?"

"Yeah. We ended up having a visitor a few hours ago. He came early."

Lacy's mom turned the corner and, to her surprise,

saw Nathan sitting in the chair next to the fire in his dress blues.

"Oh my. Nathan, sorry I wasn't here when you got here. I was expecting you later tonight."

"Yes. It seems that I arrived early. Some of the boys from the base dropped me off."

"Oh, no worries. I just didn't know. I would have let my daughter know."

"Yes, mom, it was quite a surprise." Lacy rolled her eyes and gave her mom a look.

"Sorry." But she could not help but crack a smile, already seeing how this stranger made her daughter smile again. "Nathan, it is great to meet you. If you will excuse me for a moment, I will be right back down."

While her mom was upstairs, the two continued their conversation.

"So, before we were interrupted, I was going to ask you one last question," Lacy said.

"Go for it."

"What do you want to do when you retire?"

"I am hoping to become a trauma nurse."

"Oh, that will keep you on your toes. You have a thrill for adventure or something?" "Maybe just a little. Do you?" he said with a smile from ear to ear.

"Not as much as you, I think, but I do like to try new things. I've started to try new foods and drinks recently. You could say I am starting to be more adventurous with some things."

"Well, that is a start."

They were interrupted again as they heard foot-steps coming down the stairs.

"Well, both of you must have had time to get ac-quainted," her mom said.

"We have," Lacy and Nathan said in unison.

"I hate to interrupt, but I could really use some help with dinner. Y'all up for it?" Stephanie, her mom, asked.

They walked into the kitchen, and her mom asked some questions delaying preparation for dinner.

"Okay, well, it looks like I missed a lot," her mom said.

"Well, I was here for four hours," Nathan explained.

"Oh, you came really early!"

"Mom, you already said that. It was fine... we kept busy talking, and the time flew by."

"Oh well, then I'm glad you felt welcomed."

"How could I not? Your daughter is very welcoming."

"Okay, both of you, can we just get to work?" Lacy exclaimed. She never really liked compliments, and she still felt uncomfortable about another man other than her fiancé flirting or being nice to her in that way.

"Lacy, we were just talking. Did you hear any word?" her mom interrupted her thoughts.

"Oh, sorry, I was thinking about something."

"We were saying that we need to start on the pies for the evening. I am going to take care of dinner tonight, and I want you and Nathan to make the pies."

"Okay. I am just going to take a quick break, and I'll be back in fifteen minutes." "Is everything okay?" her mom asked.

"Yeah, Mom, I just need a second," Lacy said as she turned, trying to hide her tears.

Lacy left the kitchen and headed outside. She felt like she was slowly having her memories of her fiancé slip out of her mind, and she did not want to let him go. She felt that if she let another man into her life, it would not be fair to her late fiancé. She walked down the sidewalk to the local graveyard. She headed to the gravestone with her fiancé's name engraved on it: *James Townson.*

Chapter Three

When she got to his gravesite, the tears began to flow, and she laid down on the grass right beside it. On his gravestone, the quote, "Always remembered," and his favorite Bible verse, Psalm 23, were engraved on the stone. Each year she came to his gravesite, and she spent time talking to him as if he were still there to listen.

"Hello, sweetheart. So, it has been five years now, and every day I feel that it gets easier, but I miss you every day. I think this year, it is actually hitting me a little harder because my mom invited someone for Thanksgiving, and he reminds me of you. And I'm not going to lie, I felt something that I never thought I could feel after you. I feel that I might be able to fall in love again even though my heart aches for you always."

Lacy stayed there another hour. She lost track of time. She always did when she came to talk to him. She glanced at her watch and realized she needed to head back home. The sky started to light up with pink, purple, and yellow colors as the sun went down. It would be getting dark soon, and she realized that it would probably be best to get back home before dark.

I should go back soon, Lacy thought.

As she was thinking this, she stood on her feet and began walking back when she noticed someone standing in the distance. "Nathan, how long have you been here for?"

"Well, to be honest, I followed you because I was worried. I didn't overhear anything, and I went back to the house after I saw that it was a private moment."

"So, then you came back?"

'Yeah...after an hour, your mom got worried. Also, your dad got home a few minutes ago, and it is time to eat dinner."

"Oh, no. I'm sorry. I always lose track of time when I go here."

"Are you ready to head back to the house, or do you want me to leave?"

"No... I am ready to go, and after all, we still have to make those pies tonight."

"You're right. Those pies won't bake themselves."

Nathan and Lacy walked back together. Although the conversation came so easily before, this time, their walk was filled only with the sound of raindrops falling and their own footsteps on the ground. The rain started to come down faster, and neither of them was prepared. It was like it came out of nowhere. There were no gray clouds, and the weather did not call for rain anytime soon. They started to run as the light drizzle turned into a downpour. The downpour luckily came as they were in sight of her house. As Lacy ran alongside Nathan up the driveway, she slipped from the wetness of the rain and fell on her backside. She could not help but laugh, which broke the silence. Nathan joined her in laughter as he came up to her.

"Are you okay?" he said, concerned but also still laughing.

"Yeah, I am fine," Lacy replied between winces of pain.

He took her hand and helped her back up to her feet. Then they walked the rest of the way slowly up the driveway to the front door. At the front door, Nathan and Lacy tried to get as much water out of their clothes before entering the house. A puddle was left on the porch as they finished wringing out the water. Nathan could still see the pain in Lacy's eyes. He was concerned for her, and he wanted to help her out in any way he could.

"I can see how much pain you are in right now. If you want, I can just tell your parents you aren't feeling well, and I can take care of the pies," Nathan said, trying to let her know he cared.

"I appreciate that. I needed the time, and now I'm ready." She was surprised how much he cared when he barely knew her.

"Are you sure?"

"I'm sure."

They walked back into the house and headed upstairs to change out of their soaking wet clothes.

Lacy changed into a sweatshirt and sweatpants

to help her warm up from the cold rain outside. Nathan followed behind her up the stairs and walked to his room. He changed into sweatpants and a t-shirt. He had his dress blues on all day, and now they stuck to him from the waterfall of rain his clothes absorbed.

Lacy came downstairs first and talked to her dad with just a little time before they would sit down for dinner.

"Dad, it is so good to see you!"

"Lacy, I am so glad to see you. It feels like it has been a long time," her dad said as he came in for a hug. His other little girl was home, and he was so happy.

A few minutes later, Nathan came back downstairs and walked back into the kitchen, looking much comfier. Lacy looked up from her conversation with her father. Nathan stood at the bottom of the stairs staring at her. As much as she thought he looked good in his blues, it was nothing to compare to him looking rugged in his sweatpants and his disheveled wet hair. She stared back at him as if they were the only two in the room. Nathan continued to keep eye contact with Lacy until he approached her father and introduced himself.

"Hello, sir. My name is Nathan. Thank you for having me over for Thanksgiving," Nathan said nervously.

"Nathan, it is a pleasure to have you here. I'm Micah. Thank you for coming," Lacy's dad replied.

Just as they finished with introductions, Lacy's mom announced that dinner was ready. The table was set, and the four of them sat down for dinner. Her mom made pizza for dinner, knowing that the next day would be filled with many different foods. The pizza was simple with just cheese and pepperoni. Lacy's dad asked everyone to bow their heads for prayer. They were all so hungry, so he made the prayer short and sweet. Lacy closed her eyes, but not before she watched Nathan. She knew it might not tell her if he was a Christian, but she wanted to see if he would at least respect prayer time.

The pizza was so cheesy and yummy that everyone was enjoying it. Not a word was spoken. In between Lacy's dad's third slice, he asked Nathan a question.

"So, Nathan, how long have you been in the service?"

"Ten years now. I told Lacy earlier that I plan to stay in for a few more years and then retire."

"Well, I want to personally say thank you for all you do. We are glad to have you these few days but sorry that you couldn't spend this time with your family. Consider us your family now." "Thank you, sir. That is incredibly nice of you to say."

"I mean it."

"Well, thank you. So, I talked with Lacy, but we never got to talking about what you do."

Lacy and her mom ate and just listened while the two men talked to each other. They thought that maybe they should let the men do the talking for a change.

"I'm actually a ME, Medical Examiner, for the police department and work with the detectives on the cases."

"That is so fascinating."

"Yes, it is an adventure each day. It never gets old."

Lacy's mom intervened. "Yeah, he can't tell us much, but when he does, it always fascinates me. I mean, I know I cannot be a wife who visits her husband at work because, well, you know, it wouldn't be the best place to eat lunch." The rest of them chuckled.

"Yeah, makes sense. So, what would be one of the stories that you could tell?" Nathan said with a chuckle.

"Well, I can't really say anything about the cases or the people... but what I can say is that it is interesting that some murderers don't make a plan for murder and are so much easier to find. While, on the other hand, others plan the murder so well that it's almost impossible to find the killer."

"Honey, you are a little quiet over there. Are you okay?" Lacy's dad said with concern in his eyes.

"Yeah, dad. I just want to listen tonight, and I got the opportunity to talk to Nathan already, so I'm letting y'all talk and learn more about him."

After all, Lacy told the truth; she just did not have much energy to talk. She wanted to get the dinner over with and go to bed.

"Okay. I was just making sure. You know that you can leave the table and excuse yourself if you need to at any time. We will all understand."

"Okay, Dad. Nathan and I are still needing to make the pies, and I really want to help do that, so I'm okay."

At the dinner table, Lacy's parents and Nathan continued talking while Lacy sat back watching. After fifteen minutes, Lacy and her mom excused themselves to go to the kitchen and do the dishes. Lacy's dad and Nathan stayed at the table. Nathan felt a little nervous, wondering if her dad would ask him more questions. He knew that this was not a typical situation, and he was not here to meet the parents, but he still wondered what her dad would ask with only the two left in the room.

"Nathan, I know that you are only here until tomorrow, but I can see how you look at my daughter," her dad said. "Now that it's just us, can you tell me if you have any intentions of what will happen after you leave?"

"Yes, sir. I thought it was pretty obvious. Honestly, that is up to her because I would love to even just have a friendship for now, but I'm not exactly sure how she feels about it. It might be too early for her."

"So, she told you?"

"Yes, sir. She said I would find out tomorrow, and she wanted to tell me beforehand to get it out of the way."

"I think... that I cannot speak for her, but I hope that she is getting to the point where she could fall in love again. I can see how even this year, she is smiling more. Maybe it is more healing, but I think that it might be more because of you."

"Do you really think so?"

"Yes. I have only seen her in love once, and I'm not saying she is in love, but I can see that she might be interested."

"Thank you for making me aware. I would like to date her if she would be open to it. You know this makes me feel like I'm back in high school getting permission before being able to date someone."

"Good. I'm glad you are nervous," Lacy's dad said, trying not to chuckle.

There was a brief moment of silence before Lacy's father continued talking.

"I'm just kidding. You have nothing to be nervous about. I think the only thing I am concerned about is that your being in the military would hold her back from pursuing anything with you. I don't want my sweet daughter to be hurt again. I know I can't do anything to protect her from that, and it scares me knowing that it could happen again."

"I was thinking about that too, sir, and that is why I haven't said anything to her. I understand if she doesn't want to risk the chance of that happening again."

"Well, I know that it is beyond the time that you need my permission to date my daughter, but regardless, you are a good man that I can see. I want you to know I give you my blessing to date her."

"Thank you, sir. It means a lot to me."

The conversation in the dining room continued as another conversation between Lacy and her mom started in the kitchen.

"So, Lacy, you can't tell me that there isn't something there with you and Nathan. When I interrupted you guys talking at the fireplace, I would have never known that you weren't a couple."

"Okay, Mom, you are right, but I don't know if I can do it again. I like him, and he is the first man who has made me feel anything since James. I just don't know if I can start something with him still being on active duty. The same thing could happen again, and I don't think that I could stand it a second time. I think it would completely break me."

"I understand that, Lacy...but also, if you don't, you could miss out on so much. I can see how he brings a light into you that I haven't seen since James. You are still so young, and I know that you can find love again."

"Can we not talk about love right now and maybe just talk about chemistry? I'm not ready to love someone again like that."

"Maybe not now... but as time goes on, I hope you do let someone back into your life."

They finished putting the last few dishes in the dishwasher and scrubbing the pizza pan clean. Lacy's mom walked back into the dining room to say goodnight. Lacy's dad followed suit and said goodnight, too.

"We should probably get to making those pies. I'm really tired, and tomorrow is going to be a long day," Lacy tried to say in the nicest way to Nathan.

"Yeah, you are probably right. Let's get to it."

Nathan and Lacy found all the ingredients in the pantry and put them all on the kitchen island. Once all of the ingredients were out, they decided who would make the crusts and work on the filling. Lacy got out some aprons so that all the mess would stay off their clothes.

Lacy started to work on the crust for both pies. Nathan stared at her as he started on the filling. He looked at her as flour landed on the left side of her forehead and in her hair. A picture of what the future could be popped in his head. Lacy looked up as he was glancing at her. They both stared at each other for a moment. Once again, she could not believe how much Nathan reminded her of James in looks and personality.

Could I get lucky again to find someone like this? she thought.

Nathan thought about her, too. *Will she ever be able to love me?*

After procrastinating, he grabbed all the ingredients and focused on making the apple pie and pumpkin pie filling. He did not have to do much except put the apples in a cinnamon-sugar mix in a bowl and mix it around. Then for the pumpkin filling, all he had to do was take it out of the can. While he mixed those concoctions together, Lacy worked hard on making the dough. In the time in between, when the dough needed to chill, Nathan and Lacy both sat down at the table to take a load off their aching feet. Their talking resumed where they left off earlier that day.

"So, while we wait, tell me more about why you want to be a trauma nurse."

"I think to sum it up... I would say because of the excitement in the field as a corpsman for the Marines that I wouldn't be able to do a job that is slower. I like staying on my feet, and I think that being a trauma nurse will do that. I also have a lot of experience over the years, and I think I could bring a lot to whatever I end up in."

"Well, you don't have to sell the idea to me. It seems like that is something you will love to do."

"What about you? Do you want to stay in Kansas and continue your event planning there?"

"I've thought about moving back. I would be a lot closer to my family, and I would love that...but I'm not sure if I'm ready to do that just yet. I think... like you, it would be in a few years until I move home. I have a growing business in Kansas, and moving back would mean starting all over."

"Well, I know that you could find so many clients here or wherever you go."

The conversation flowed for the next hour until the dough was chilled. Nathan went to get it from the fridge and then realized that he had no clue what he was doing. Nathan never made a crust for pie before. Lacy took the bowl of dough from his hand, put flour on the counter, and started rolling it out before thinking it would be fun to teach Nathan how to make the crust.

"Nathan, do you want me to show you how to make the crust?" Lacy excitedly asked.

"I would like that," Nathan smiled back.

She moved away from the dough and let Nathan take her place. Then she came behind him and took his hands so that they could work together on rolling out the dough. She guided her hands on his as they rolled the dough to the correct thickness. Nathan could hear his heart beating so fast. It was like the bass on the radio, so loud that literally anyone could hear it. He slowly turned his head within inches of Lacy's face. They stopped at that moment, staring at each other until the oven preheat alarm went off. The moment was over. Lacy backed away from whatever could have happened. She could not believe that she had put herself in that slippery situation.

"Nathan, I'm sorry I just did that. I hope it didn't make you feel uncomfortable. It was not my intention. I don't want to give you missed signals, and I honestly don't know if I am ready yet.

I'm sorry for confusing you."

"I understand, and this is on your terms. I think that we should just develop a friendship, and when you are ready, we could pursue something more."

"Agreed."

They left it at that. Lacy finished putting the lattice on top of the pie and then put both pies in the oven. Nathan headed off to bed and said goodnight as Lacy waited for the pies to be done. It was ironic that she was the most tired, yet she was the last to sleep. She took a nap on the couch until the oven dinged, telling her the pies were done. She checked to make sure they were done and then put the tins on a cooling rack where they would stay overnight. Half asleep, she walked up the stairs to her room, landed on her comfortable bed, and within about five minutes fell asleep. It felt like sleeping on a cloud. The last thing she remembered thinking about was how Thanksgiving would be different with Nathan in the house as her eyes shut and she drifted off to sleep.

Chapter Four

Lacy woke up a few hours later. She had trouble sleeping. Every time she closed her eyes, she heard the knock on the door, and every time she woke up, she remembered that James was gone. It was like a haunting reoccurring dream that would never go away. The memories would come back, but she had never experienced them this consistently before. She did not want to sleep or close her eyes anymore. The memory yesterday already replayed in her mind so many times, and she did not know how much longer she could take it. Lacy walked down the stairs to a house filled with darkness with a little bit of light shining through the window from the sunrise. She grabbed her coat off the hook in the hallway and opened the door as quietly as she could without waking anyone upstairs. She tiptoed out of the house and shut the door behind her. The door creaked slightly, but not enough to wake anyone in the house. Finally, she ran down the drive and back to the gravesite as fast as she could. Usually, she would only visit James' gravesite once a year, but something drew her back to it again this year. She walked up to his stone and lay on the ground. The ground had a cover of dew, and she could feel tiny droplets attaching to her skin and clothes from the grass.

"Hi, James. You are probably surprised that I'm back so soon. I don't know if it is because I'm feeling guilty about moving on, but I need to let this go. The memories will forever be on my mind, but I can't have them haunting me anymore. I love you and always will... but last night, I was reminded of how love could feel from someone else. James, you have my heart, but I'm ready to give another piece of my heart to someone else soon."

After spending another two hours just lying there and praying, Lacy got up and headed back to the house. On the way, tiny snowflakes started to fall from the sky, snowflakes that each had an individual design. As she continued to walk, the flurries became bigger and bigger, and the wind blew faster. She rushed back up the drive and into the house. When she walked back into the house, there was the smell of something scrumptious in the oven. It smelled of chocolate and a hint of cinnamon. She tiptoed into the kitchen to find her mom sitting down, drinking a cup of coffee and doing a word search.

"Good morning, mom!"

"Good morning. I did not know you were up. You went somewhere in your pajamas?"

"Oh, I didn't even realize. Well, no one was out there this morning, so I guess it didn't matter."

"Did you go to James' gravesite again?"

"Yes, mom, but don't worry. Last night, I could not sleep, and I went to talk to him. I prayed for two hours or so, and God began to give me peace about the past and also my current situation. I think that soon I will be ready to let someone love me again."

"Well, I'm glad. I got worried last night when you barely talked. I came down to get something I forgot last night and saw you helping him roll out the dough. I could see how you are slowly letting your guard down. But as your mom, I also worry if you should get in a relationship with someone right now."

"You don't have to worry… there is no relationship other than a friendship in my near future."

"Good. You know I'm just looking out for you, sweetie."

"By the way, Mom, the muffins smell so good as always. When they get out of the oven, please save me some. I'm going to head upstairs and take a shower after getting drenched in water from all the dew. I can't wait to get nice and warm."

On the way upstairs, Lacy did not look up. She figured no one else could be up at such an early hour. She did not look in the mirror, but she knew that her hair was a mess. On her way up the stairs, she accidentally bumped into Nathan on his way down for breakfast. In just a split second, Nathan slid down on his back, and Lacy's feet slipped underneath her. It left them on top of each other and within inches of each other's faces for the second time in less than 24 hours.

The only thing Lacy's mom heard was the thud of Nathan falling, and then all was silent until laughter broke the silence.

"Wow, we have to stop meeting like this," Nathan said with a chuckle in his voice.

"You are telling me! Are you okay? I'm so sorry I didn't see where I was going."

"I think I will be okay, but I'm going to have to watch out when I'm around you," Nathan said with a smile on his face that said it all.

"Okay, I think we should get up."

"Do we have to just yet?"

Before Lacy could answer, they heard footsteps, and that answered Nathan's question.

"Okay, just kidding. I'm getting up before I'm caught by your mom."

"Good to know. I'll see you soon. By the way, I am loving the pajamas." His red and black plaid flannel pajamas reminded Lacy of fall and Christmas all wrapped into one. They resembled one of the blankets in the living room. Lacy teased him, but she also thought that he looked really handsome in the flannel.

"I could say the same to you," he said, noticing her fleece snowman pajamas.

Lacy had just made it up the stairs and to her room as her mom made her way to the bottom of the stairs. Like any mother would do, she would get to the bottom of this by simply asking Nathan what happened.

"Nathan, I heard a thud on the stairs and laughter. Is everything okay?"

"Oh, yes, ma'am. We just had a mishap and ran into each other, which led us to both falling on the stairs."

"And both of you are okay?"

"Yes, we are more than okay."

"Well, then come into the kitchen and get some muffins I just made. Also, I saw the pies from last night."

Nathan's face perked up as he smelled the aroma coming from the kitchen. He followed Stephanie into the kitchen, eager to see if the muffins tasted as good as they smelled.

"Wow, these are amazing muffins," Nathan said as he took a bite into one.

"Well, make sure you don't eat all of them. These are Lacy's favorite, so she will not be happy if you eat them all."

"I can see why they are her favorite. On another note, when is the rest of your family supposed to get here?"

"They will be here around 11 am, so a few hours. Don't worry, though."

"I have nothing to worry about... especially if they are anything like you guys."

Nathan took another muffin after he finished his first. Each bite he took somehow got even better. It was like eating a slice of autumn all wrapped up into one bite. He felt so much at home. In previous years, he would spend Thanksgiving on the base with the other men and women. It was nice to be with them, but something about being around family made it better.

While Nathan enjoyed the muffins, Lacy got ready for the day. She took a nice twenty-minute shower and then worked on her hair. Usually, she did not care what her hair looked like and would only do something with it for special occasions. There might have been a little extra push since Nathan came for Thanksgiving, and even with all her questions swimming around in her head, she still wanted to make a good impression. She brushed and blow-dried her hair. She thought about curling it but then remembered how it would get ruined at the annual football game. She finished with her hair and then moved to her bedroom to finish getting dressed.

She picked out a maroon jumpsuit that went down to the ankles and paired it with a gray shawl.

She looked in the mirror to see if it would be the right outfit.

"Okay, I think I'm ready," Lacy said to herself.

She opened the door to her bedroom and walked back down the stairs. This time she walked slowly downstairs, and Nathan started walking up the stairs at the same time. She saw that his pajamas had muffin crumbs all over, which meant only one thing: he ate her favorite muffins.

She could not help but stop to make a comment before she joined her mom in the kitchen.

"You know you better not have eaten all those muffins."

"I might have left you one or two. They were so good!"

"You better be joking. I planned on taking some of those back to Kansas with me!"

"I'm kidding. Your mom put some away for that reason, or I would have eaten them all."

"Phew. Good."

Lacy headed to the kitchen, pulled her apron out of the cabinet, and put it on so she could help her mom with all the side dishes. Her apron said, "Bake it until you make it." It was a present from James after being together for one year. He knew how much she loved to bake and also how she liked a play on words.

"Mom, just tell me what you need me to do, and I'm ready," Lacy said.

"Wow, honey. You look great! Yes, I need help. The stuffing needs to be made and the mashed potatoes. We will eat around noon, so you don't need to get to work quite yet. I could use your help, though, with making some rolls. You know you always love to make the bread as much as you like to eat it."

"I am on it."

Lacy got the ingredients out of the pantry for the rolls. She made sure that the apron covered her whole jumpsuit to avoid any stains, at least before dinner. Then she put her hair up in a loose bun to not mess up what she had already done with her hair. She put the ingredients together in the bowl and mixed them. Then she let the dough sit for an hour or so to give it time to rise. In the meantime, she started to work on the stuffing, getting the breadcrumbs, celery, salt, pepper, chicken broth, and a secret ingredient ready.

Upstairs, Nathan picked out his outfit. He dressed in black dress pants and a maroon button-down shirt. It just so happened he would be matching Lacy. It was the only nice clothes other than the dress blues that he brought. He looked in the mirror to see his disheveled hair and took a comb to it. While he finished up, he called his parents over video chat. He took his phone and dialed their number. Before long, his parents answered the call, and the little square in the corner showed their faces smiling right back at him.

"Hi, Mom and Dad."

"Hi, Nathan!" said Nathan's mom, Lucy. "Greetings from Missouri! Wish you could be home with us! How are you doing? Is the family nice?"

"Yes, they make me feel at home. It couldn't have been a better situation. Also, I might have gotten more than I could have ever expected...."

"Well, tell us!"

"Well, their daughter came home for Thanksgiving, and there is so much chemistry there. I really like her. I know it has only been one day, but I feel that she could be my wife someday."

"Wow. You may be right…You got more than you bargained for." "I did," he said with a big smile on his face.

"Well, then, we can't wait to meet her someday soon!"

"You might have to wait a little bit. She has a lot that happened in her past, and it isn't going to be the easiest for her to be in a relationship right away."

"Okay, just be patient. God's timing is always right."

"So other than that, how are you guys doing?"

"We are doing good but wish that you were here with us."

"Is it just going to be you and Dad? Or is Aunt Lanie coming?"

"Aunt Lanie will be over today. You know, with you being the only child, Thanksgiving has always been something small for us. Are you going to experience a big Thanksgiving meal?"

"Yes, I think so. It is her and her parents and then her siblings with their significant others. I mean, it won't be overwhelming, but it will be a bigger amount than we have ever had. It will probably be like when I've had Thanksgiving dinner on base or overseas."

"I'm sure the rest of her family will be as welcoming as they have been so far. I can really see how much you like this girl. It is written all over your face."

"Yes, she is something special."

"Well, I hope you have a great Thanksgiving and keep us updated. Love you," his mom said.

"Don't let her get away. Love you," said his dad, C.J.

"Love you both."

They hung up the video chat, and Nathan looked at the clock hanging in the room. It was one of those clocks that still had the different roman numerals on it and looked more antique than anything. He saw that it was now almost 10 o'clock. He needed to go back downstairs and see what he could do to help. He walked back into the kitchen and saw Lacy hard at work. Her mom had left the room to wake up her husband, so it was once again just Lacy and Nathan in the room.

"Wow, it looks like you've worked hard to get all this food done."

"Pretty much nonstop," Lacy said. She looked up, and she was speechless. It seemed that every time she saw him in a different outfit, he looked even better. He looked good in just about anything.

"You look nice," Lacy said to Nathan.

"I wanted to say it earlier, but you look beautiful."

After he said that, Lacy smiled and put her head down.

"You know you don't seem to take my compliments well," Nathan said.

"I'm sorry. I don't mean to be offensive. I never take

it well. I'm trying to do better."

"Well, over time, you will just have to get used to it."

"I'll try."

"So, is there anything I can do to help?"

"I think that everything is pretty much covered. You are a guest; you can just get comfortable and relax for the next few hours."

"Relaxing isn't as easy as you think."

"I can imagine. I have to work on that, too. I'm almost done, so if you want to wait a few minutes, then we can go for a walk before the whole family comes."

"That would be nice. I'll go get my shoes on."

Lacy took the rolls out of the oven and put them on a cooling rack. Lacy grabbed her shoes from the shoe rack near the front door and her shawl from the closet door in the hallway before returning to the kitchen to clean up her mess. She left the rolls on the cooling rack, knowing her mom would take care of them when she came back downstairs. Then she put her tennis shoes on. It was a little chilly outside, so she also grabbed her shawl and draped it over her shoulder. She covered her shoulders, making sure that no bare skin would be exposed. Nathan came down the stairs in light green tennis shoes and joined her in the kitchen.

"Are you ready to go?"

"I am. Those tennis shoes go great with your outfit," Lacy teased.

"Yeah, yeah. I know, but would I really rather wear

my dress shoes and be uncomfortable?"

"No, I understand."

They walked around the neighborhood. It was a relatively big neighborhood, so it would take at least 30 minutes to walk the whole thing. As they walked, they took in the beautiful fall leaves. Some houses had Christmas lights up. The lights were not lit since it was the middle of the day, but something about Christmas lights brightened up Lacy's day. They walked in silence for half the walk until Nathan gained the courage to ask Lacy something.

"Lacy, I wondered if we could stay in contact after this. I know that you need more time, but I cherish this friendship we have started, and I would like for it to continue."

"I would really like that, and thank you for being willing to understand."

They exchanged emails and phone numbers. As they approached the house after their walk, two cars were parked in the driveway.

"Well, it looks like my brother and sister both got here a little bit earlier. It seems to be a recurring pattern these days. Don't worry… you have nothing to worry about."

They walked through the front door, and the house no longer seemed as quiet. There was laughter in the kitchen and the sound of the radio on in the family room. He got ready for this big Thanksgiving adventure to begin. As he daydreamed, Lacy left his side and hurried over to her sister and brother to give them both a warm, welcoming hug. She talked with them a little before they commented about the mystery man standing in the family room.

"Um, Lacy, who is that over there?" her siblings asked in unison.

"He is the service member that Mom invited for Thanksgiving dinner. He came yesterday early. I got to talk to him yesterday before everyone else got home."

"Yeah, I'll say... it seems that he is getting to know you pretty well," said Quinn, her older brother.

"Both of you, stop it. We are just friends. I'll admit, though, I wasn't expecting this, especially at this time of year."

"Well, I am glad that someone is making you smile again," her sister said.

"Well, let me introduce you."

Lacy walked back over to him and asked him if he was ready to meet the rest of her family. "Yes," Nathan said.

Lacy walked over with him to his sister first, who was with her fiancé.

"Nathan, this is my younger sister, Hannah, and her fiancé, Cody."

"It is nice to meet you, Nathan."

Then she moved on to the kitchen to introduce him to her brother and his wife.

"And Nathan, this is my brother, Quinn, and his wife, Catherine." "It is nice to meet you!" they both said.

Quinn stopped Nathan in his tracks, ready to quiz him with hard questions about his intentions when their mother announced that dinner was ready.

"I see that everyone has met Nathan. He is the service member that we invited for Thanksgiving.

I came to say that dinner is served and everything is ready. Let's go eat."

The whole family headed into the dining room. The table was decked with a festive fall tablecloth and in the middle, as the centerpiece, was the delicious turkey. The turkey looked like it was cooked just right, and each side dish completed the meal.

Lacy's dad interrupted the conversation going on at the table. "Alright, everyone, we are going to hold hands around the table as I say the blessing."

It just so happened that Lacy and Nathan got placed right next to each other at the table. If she did not know any better, Lacy would have thought that her mom did that on purpose. She tried to focus on the prayer, but instead, her body shook from the touch of his hand. She tried to not think about it, and soon the moment would be over. As the prayer finished, everyone grabbed their forks, and the food was served. On the table was the turkey in the middle, stuffing on one side, a corn casserole, and rolls in a basket. They passed the food to the right so that everyone got a chance to get what they wanted to eat. Conversation flew between everyone, and eventually, the questions came to Nathan. Lacy's siblings could not take the suspense any longer. They knew why he was here, but they wanted to know more about him. Even though both her siblings were younger than Lacy, they still looked out for her.

"So, Nathan, tell us about yourself," said Quinn. "Have you ever been in a relationship before?"

Lacy cut in. "Guys, stop. You don't need to bother him with those questions. Ask him something different."

Nathan answered anyway. "No, I have not been in a relationship before. I've been close, but it never worked out. I've been on a few dates, and that's all."

Lacy interrupted again. "Nathan, you don't need to answer anymore."

"It's fine."

Hannah chimes in. "Okay, so why is that?"

"I've always been away, and I never wanted to get into a relationship while I was in the service. I thought about it and was going to be open to it, but it never worked out, and I was okay with that. The only thing that could change my mind is someone special who I knew could weather the storm with me. I just never found someone who could take me being in the military."

"So, there are no other reasons we should know about?" Quinn asked.

"Okay, guys, seriously, stop. He didn't come here to get grilled. You aren't making him feel welcome," Lacy said with an irritated tone in her voice.

"No," Nathan answered. He didn't mind at first, but now he was the center of the conversation. He wished that someone would change the subject and get the attention off of him. He was very grateful for Lacy trying to take the conversation somewhere else.

Lacy came up with a way to change the subject that she hoped would work. "Nathan, I know you can't talk a lot about your job, but I would like to hear any stories you do have."

He took her hint and began talking.

"Well, I would start with boot camp. It was a really difficult time, but I met a lot of people who I will have relationships with for a lifetime. It was nothing like I've ever experienced before. There were days when I wanted to give up. In the end, I couldn't believe that boot camp was over, and I made it through. I went home feeling like a brand-new man, and I hadn't even been deployed yet. I don't really like to talk about what I've had to experience over there, but what I can say is that each service member I've helped is what makes me continue to want to do it."

There was silence in the room. No one knew what to say. Hannah and Quinn got embarrassed.

"Nathan, we want to apologize," said Hannah. "We didn't mean to make you feel uncomfortable."

"Yes," added Quinn. "We are very sorry."

"I forgive you. I know that you are all trying to look

out for Lacy and be protective of her.”

After that, the conversation turned from talking about Nathan to him asking questions to Lacy's siblings.

“So, Hannah, when did you and Cody meet?”

Hannah started sharing their story. “We met in college a few years ago. He was in the class before me, and I always got there early for my class. I walked to the place where I would sit in the class, and someone was still in my seat packing up. I could have made it awkward by just standing there and waiting for my chair, but instead, I came up to him and started talking to him.”

“Yeah, she asked why I chose that specific seat,” Cody said. “At first, I was like, *how is this beautiful woman even talking to me right now*? I felt like I was on air when she talked with me. She explained how she always sat in that spot and was just trying to break the ice.”

“And after asking that, I thought, *why did I just ask him such a weird question*? I second-guessed everything and was about to turn around and go somewhere else to sit down.”

“That is when I got out of my chair and pulled it out for her to sit down,” Cody explained. “I said something pretty corny, and then I took the chance and asked her if we could meet after class.”

“And the rest is history because I said yes.”

“We are in our last year at college, so once we graduate, we will get married in August. I'm going to be working as an accountant, and Hannah will be going to veterinarian school," Cody added.

"That is very exciting! Congratulations! And what about you, Quinn and Catherine?" Nathan said, turning to give them his attention.

Catherine spoke for both of them. "We actually work together flipping houses together. We've done that for a few years, and it's now our full-time work."

"Wow, that sounds amazing. I can't wait to hear more about it and see some of your work." "Actually, since we are on the subject of us… We have some news," Catherine said.

Then, both in unison, Catherine and Quinn made their announcement. "We are expecting a baby!"

"Oh, my gosh!" everyone screamed!

"This is the best thing ever! I'm going to be an aunt!" Lacy exclaimed with the excitement of someone in the candy store as a child.

The rest of the time at the dinner table, they talked about preparations for Hannah and Cody's wedding and Catherine and Quinn's baby arriving. Both siblings asked Lacy to plan the wedding and the baby shower. That meant she would be back in Virginia even more than usual. She knew how important family was, and there was no way that she would pass off the job to anybody else. She also thought that maybe this would be the foot in the door for moving her business back to

Virginia in the next few years. Conversation continued to flow at the table, and now it was the kind of conversation and feeling that Nathan always imagined.

They finished up with dinner, and then Lacy and her sister cleared off the table. There were a lot of dishes, so Nathan got up and helped carry the rest of the dirty dishes into the kitchen. Lacy worked on loading up the dishwasher as much as she could and then finished up scrubbing the pots that would not fit in the dishwasher. It might sound crazy, but doing the dishes in a way was therapeutic, with the soap and suds covering her hands. While she did that, the rest of the family moved from the dining room and went upstairs to change into workout clothes. Nathan got confused about what was happening, so he stayed in the kitchen to help Lacy dry the dishes. He had a question on the tip of his tongue, but before he could ask, Lacy answered his question.

"Nathan. I think my family forgot to tell you, but we do an annual football game every year after our dinner, which is why they are all changing their clothes right now. We clean up and let our food digest a little and then head to the backyard for the game."

"Okay, everything makes sense now." Nathan finished drying the dishes and then headed upstairs to change. Luckily, he had brought one more pair of clothes just in case he went straight from the dinner to work out on the base. He changed into a T-shirt and shorts that both had the Navy logo. He also put his green sneakers back on. He thought *This is going to be fun! I've never played a football game with my family before. I wonder how they play or if anyone is good.*

He headed back downstairs and to the backyard, where the rest of the family warmed up for the game. He stepped onto the grass and joined everyone else.

What am I getting myself into? he thought as he began stretching his quads and looking at the serious expressions painted on their faces.

Chapter Five- The Game

Everyone was outside except for Lacy and her mom. They finished cleaning the last dishes and headed upstairs to change into workout clothes for the football game. Lacy put on a long sleeve compression shirt and then paired the shirt with black shorts. She ran down the stairs and out to the backyard to see everyone doing a warm-up lap around the yard.

"Sorry, we are a little late."

"Yeah. We were thinking that you guys would miss out on the game," said Micah, Lacy's dad.

"Well, we are here now. We are ready if you guys are."

Everyone said in unison with excitement in their voices, "Let's play!"

First, the captains got picked. Cody was chosen as the captain of one team, and Lacy's dad was the other captain. Then the captains chose who they wanted on their team. Cody went first and chose Hannah. He did not want to compete against her, so he wanted her on his team. Lacy's dad picked Quinn. Then Cody chose again, and he chose Lacy. Lacy's dad chose Nathan, and Cody chose Lacy's mom. Lacy's dad chose Catherine; she was less than a month along, so she still wanted to be a part of the game. She would just be more cautious than usual.

The backyard was large but probably only half the size of a football field. The game was so intense that a few days beforehand, the family would go outside and use spray paint to put down the yard lines and first downs. Since it was a combination of skill levels, the family decided that two-hand touch was the best way to go. Lacy's dad set a timer for each quarter on his phone, only pausing it for timeouts. He placed it on the sidelines on a chair so that everybody could see the time running down.

Cody's team got to have the ball first. As a team, Cody's team picked him to be the quarterback. The other team kicked off, and the ballgame began. On the kickoff, Hannah caught the ball and ran for a gain of 5. Then for the second down, Lacy's mom caught the ball but did not get many yards before she was stopped by Lacy's dad. They were now at third down. The team got into a huddle to discuss a play. Then Cody caught the snapped ball and threw the ball to the 10-yard line. It was a high throw and almost impossible to catch. Lacy saw the ball coming, and she reached out to grab it. It toppled a little, but then she was able to gain control of the ball. Nathan was in charge of blocking her. He was right behind her when she caught the ball. As she caught the ball, she fell to the ground along with Nathan. He fell first, and then she fell on him. There was not much movement for a minute. The family gathered around them to make sure everyone was okay. After another minute, Lacy made a comment to Nathan, and he laughed.

"Okay, we have to stop doing this. I mean, it is the second time today," Lacy chuckled.

"I know."

"Are you okay?"

"Yes, I'm enjoying this moment."

"That is what you said before."

"I know. It's the truth."

"Maybe we should get up. We are going to get a penalty for a delay of game."

"Okay…okay… ruin the fun again."

Lacy got up first, and then she put out her hand to help Nathan up. He grabbed her hand and stood to his feet. They could see everyone surrounding them, and as they got up, Nathan exclaimed, "We are okay. We just got the wind knocked out of us for a moment."

"Good."

They waited another five minutes, and then the game continued. Cody's team got the 1st down, and it was first and goal. Cody passed the ball off to Lacy's mom, and she got a few yards short of the end zone. Now it was 2nd down, Cody passed off the ball again, and Hannah grabbed the ball, missed the blockers, and ran into the end zone. Touchdown! Now it was 6-0. Since they did not have goal posts, there would be no extra point. Instead, they would automatically go for two points each time. The team lined up, Cody passed the ball to Hannah, and Catherine blocked her.

No extra points.

Lacy kicked off the ball, and Nathan caught it on the other team. He somehow slipped through the blocker and got almost 30 yards before he was stopped by Cody. Quinn was the quarterback on the other team. It was 1st down, and the team only had 20 yards to the end zone. The team lined up, and the ball snapped. Hannah ran up to Quinn and stopped him before he could throw the ball. Now it was 2nd down. Quinn got the ball from the snap and threw it to Lacy's dad.

Lacy's dad ran down and caught the ball with two yards to go. It was 3rd down, and the team was starting to feel the pressure. They called a timeout and huddled to discuss what play would work best. The team lined up again, and Quinn faked passing the ball. He then slipped past the defenders and made it into the end zone. The score was tied. Quinn and the team lined up to try for the extra two points. He passed the ball to Catherine, who was able to run into the end zone. The score now read 6-8. Cody and his team were two points behind. It looked like that those extra points would have been helpful.

The game continued. At halftime, the score was Cody's team 22-24. The miss of the first extra points was following Cody's team, and they were starting to worry that they would lose the game only by two. At halftime, the teams went back into the house to fill up their water bottles. Nathan crossed enemy lines to talk to Lacy with the little time they had left before halftime was over.

"I never knew what this day would hold. I can say I never imagined how much fun the day would be. And I mean, come on! A football game. Your family is very competitive."

"I hope not too competitive. And I am glad that you are enjoying your time."

"Well, some are more than others... but you all seem like you are okay at playing football."

"Well, that is thanks to my dad for playing with us as kids and our annual football game each year. My dad, Hannah, and Quinn would play all the time when we were kids. As we grew up, we continued to love the game, but it became more of us siblings. Quinn and Cody both did football in middle school and high school, as you can probably see. Did you play?"

"No, I actually played lacrosse and basketball in high school. I have played football with the boys at the base and when we have off time. Did you play any sports in school?"

"I played soccer, the closest I could get to football since my parents would never allow it... and I never would get the courage to be on a whole team of guys."

"Haha... I just pictured you on the team."

"Wait, you think that is funny?"

"No, I didn't mean it that way. I meant it was a good picture of how you could shape half the guys into shape."

"Nice save."

A person from the other room started yelling, "Okay, it is time for the second half!! Let's go, everyone!! The more we wait, the longer we have to wait for pie!"

That was the cue for everyone to grab one last sip of water and go back outside. Since Cody's team started the first half, Lacy's dad's team got to receive the second-half first. Lacy's mom kicked the ball, and it soared into the air all the way down to their 10-yard line. It would be more challenging for the team to score with the ball being placed that far back. The ball snapped, and Quinn caught it. He looked to see if anyone was open, but he could not find anyone. He tried running but actually lost yards. On 2nd down, Quinn passed the ball to Catherine and got two yards. On 3rd down, Quinn decided to throw the ball, it went a few yards in the air, and then Nathan caught it. It looked like they might get a 1st down, but Lacy was right there to stop Nathan the minute the ball landed in his hand. The team was too far away to score any points, so they decided to not go for the 4th down. Lacy's dad kicked off the ball and, on the other team, Hannah caught the ball. There was an open space between two defenders, and Hannah ran right through to get 5 yards. That meant 5 yards more to go to get a 1ˢᵗ down. Each team lined up, and the ball was snapped. Cody caught the ball and passed it off to Lacy's mom, who took it for another 5 yards getting the 1ˢᵗ down. On second down, Cody threw the ball to Lacy open 10 yards down the field. She sprinted as quickly as she could and caught the ball, ran the remainder of the yards, and down to the end zone. Her team cheered and met her in the end zone. Then they lined up for the extra points. They needed this play, and the extra points were crucial this time. Cody called a timeout. The team gathered together and talked strategy.

"What do you think we should do to get these extra points?"

Hannah shared, "I think you should throw the ball."

"I agree." Lacy and her mom said.

"Okay, Lacy, I think that you could get past Nathan and catch the ball. I am going to look for you."

"Sounds good," all of them replied.

Cody and his team lined back up. Hannah snapped the ball, and Cody caught it. Just as they thought, Lacy found an opening to get away from Nathan for a split second, and that was all she needed. She dove for the ball, and like a miracle, she caught it only being a few inches from the ground. The team cheered and came up to her to celebrate. They all high-fived each other and cheered for at least another ten seconds. The score was now 30-24. The family continued playing the rest of the

3rd quarter without either team scoring anything. In the fourth quarter, it was still a standstill. Both teams were losing energy, and it showed with neither of them scoring. The sweat dripped off of each person's shirt, and in the faint distance, wheezing could be heard from a few of the players. With two minutes left, Lacy's dad and the team got the ball.

They ran it for 1 yard, then 3 yards, and then 1 more yard. They decided to go for the 4th down and ended up short by 2 yards. Cody and the team got the ball. They just needed to hold on to the ball as long as they could and run down the clock. Cody passed the ball off to Hannah, who took it to get a 1st down. He repeated the play, and Hannah got 5 more yards. There were now only 30 seconds left. The ball was snapped, and Cody threw it high in the air. It was a perfect spiral. The ball kept on going, and Lacy kept on running to try and reach it. The ball started to come more into vision, and Lacy kept on running. She saw it coming down, and she went to grab the ball when Nathan, out of nowhere, knocked it down to the ground. The game was over. Lacy and the team lined up on the sideline and then shook the players' hands on the other team.

"Good game. Good game. Good game" echoed in the air.

The family started to flood back into the house to get more water and the reward of pie for working hard. Lacy and Nathan stayed at the back of the pack. Lacy had to tease Nathan about that last play.

"Nathan, did you really have to block that last play? Couldn't you have just let me catch it? It would have been epic."

"No. I can't just let you win," he said with a smirk on his face.

"I know, I know. But since we already were going to win, I was just thinking it would be a good story to tell."

"Sorry," he said. He was not really sorry, though. He was laughing.

"Okay, I see how it is."

Lacy and Nathan walked into the house and followed the rest of the family back to the dining room for the pie. Luckily, the smell of the pie overcame the smell of every sweaty person in the room; otherwise, the place might have smelled like a locker room. Each person got a slice of pie and vanilla ice cream. There was not much talking because everyone was enjoying the delicious pies in front of them. The silence was interrupted by the ringtone of a country song going off at medium volume. It was Nathan's phone. He got up, excused himself, and walked outside to take the call.

Chapter Six

The number on his cell phone said it all. Finally, reality sank in.

Nathan answered the phone, a bit disappointed. "Hey, bro. What's up?"

One of his friends exclaimed, "We are about five minutes away from the house to pick you up!"

"Really?" Nathan sounded annoyed.

"You don't sound excited."

"I was having a really good time."

"Well, you will have to tell us all about it when we come."

"Oh, I will!

He got off the phone and then joined everyone back in the dining room.

"Well, that was just my friends. I can't believe how fast the day went. It seems that they are on their way to pick me up in a few minutes."

"Oh my...that did go by fast. It was a pleasure to have you here. Know that you are welcome back at any time," Lacy's mom said.

"I'll take you up on that. Thank you for such a great time and experience. It will not be something I forget."

Then Lacy's dad made a comment. "Yes, Nathan, it was great to have you here. Thank you for your service, and stay safe. We hope that you know you are welcome here at any time, like my wife said."

"Yeah, man, it was great to meet you," Quinn and Cody said.

Then Hannah said, "We are sorry about earlier. It was great to meet you, and I hope to see you again."

Quinn followed with, "Yeah, sorry for my questioning earlier."

Now Lacy was the only one left to say something. They had already talked about how they would stay in touch with each other, but she tried to think of what to say to him. Lacy felt overwhelmed, so she walked out of the room, and Nathan got the cue to follow her. They were back to where it all started.

"Lacy..." Nathan hesitated.

"Sorry, Nathan. I just don't want to say goodbye, and I also don't want you to read into this. You know that I've liked getting to know you... and I feel like I've been giving you mixed signals. I want you to know I do like you... but I'm not quite ready for anything more."

"Yes, I understand. I cannot imagine what is going on in that beautiful mind of yours. I want you to know I am patient, and I will wait."

"Are you sure?"

"Yes, I am sure." he paused before sharing a story with Lacy. "One time overseas, I served someone in the

Navy. He was badly shot, and it ended up that there wasn't much that I could do to save him. I think he knew that because he told me something I will never forget. He asked me if I had ever been in love, which I replied that I really hadn't. He asked why, and I told him that I didn't want anyone to have to go through the worry and that I would wait until I was out of the military unless someone spectacular came along. Then he told me that he had someone special like that, and with his last breath, he asked me to make a promise that I would find and be open to love since he would never be able to. He died a minute later. As you can imagine, that conversation stuck with me for the longest time. Sorry for the ramble, but what I'm trying to say is that I think you could be someone who I could love, and I'm willing to wait as long as you need."

"Wow." Lacy was speechless. She did not know what to say.

"I hope I'm not scaring you."

"No, you aren't. I just didn't know what to say to that. Honestly, I think what scares me the most is the same thing happening again. I swore I would never date someone in the military again after what happened, and that is what is really holding me back right now from wanting anything more with you."

"As would be natural. And as much as I would want to promise you that I would be safe, you know I cannot promise that."

"And that is what scares me more than anything."

Nathan took Lacy's hand in his. Then he leaned in and kissed her on the forehead.

"I'm going to miss you, Lacy. I know it's only been two days, but I'm going to miss you."

"I'm going to miss you, too, Nathan. Be safe."

Then the doorbell rang. Nathan kissed Lacy on the forehead one more time before opening the door. He walked out of the door and glanced over his shoulder one last time to say goodbye.

Then just like that, he got into the car, and they drove away.

"I wonder if I will ever see him again," Lacy wondered as she joined her family back inside.

Chapter Seven

"Hey, man, what are you thinking about?" Clyde said as he looked at his friend staring into space.

"Oh, sorry, man. I just had an unforgettable day today. I was just reminiscing about everything that happened."

"Dude, we want to hear about it!" all his friends said.

The other two guys in the car from the base who came along were Martin and JJ. They persisted when Nathan did not say anything.

"Come on, we want to hear all about it, and we still have a little time before we get back to base."

"Okay. Let's just say it wasn't what I expected at all. I planned on just having a good time for Thanksgiving, but I left feeling like another part of the family."

"That is great to hear! You totally skipped over something, though. I could hear it in your voice when I talked to you on the phone," Clyde inquired.

"And you sounded excited to tell us...what changed?" asked JJ.

"I was excited to tell you. I am sorry, I think I'm just still thinking of her."

"I knew it," they all said in unison.

"Yeah...yeah."

"So, tell us all about her."

Nathan told them about everything that had happened the last few days. As he rehashed the memories, he could not help but have a smile on his face. When he finished, his friends had all kinds of questions.

Martin asked the first question. "So, what is going to happen now?"

"I'm not sure. We exchanged information, but I don't want to do anything she is not ready for." Clyde then asked a question. "But you have to do something. Man, you have been my best friend for years, and I've never seen you be this way before. She must be really special... you've got to do something. I understand respecting her wishes, but also don't just back away from it."

"I know. I just..."

All the boys again said it in unison, "No excuses, Nathan."

They arrived on base and showed their credentials to get through the gate. Before they could get on the base, there was an extra security check because of recent activities overseas. As they drove down the drive to their home away from home, Nathan thought, *My friends are right... I can't let her go.*

Clyde parked the car, and they headed in for some training before heading back to their apartment off base.

~

*L*acy spent the remainder of the day watching a movie with her family, an annual tradition along with their football game and pie. Of course, the annual movie night included popcorn, candy, and more. The whole family would snuggle together on their large couch and watch a Christmas movie. Lacy always loved this day with all their traditions. She got excited about the movie choice this year, *Home Alone*, but her mind could not help but wander the whole time the movie played.

"He kissed my forehead, and I was okay with it. Does that mean I'm actually ready and just scared?" Lacy replayed in her mind.

Her family got up to go upstairs for bed. Her sister Hannah asked her something, but at the moment, she did not hear anything.

"Hey, Lacy!" Hannah yelled.

"Oh, sorry, Hannah. My mind was somewhere else."

"Yeah, I know exactly where it is."

"I've just been wondering if I'm not willing to take the chance with Nathan, and I actually am ready to move on. But then, on the other side, I don't want to get into something too soon. You know what I mean?"

"Yes, I know what you mean. I think that right now, just continue to get to know him more and see what happens. I'm happy that you are actually seeing that you could fall in love again. It makes me really happy to see you like this again."

"Okay...thank you. I just don't want to ruin this. I do feel like it is special."

"I'll be praying for you, sis."

"Thank you. I don't know what I would do without everyone's support."

After going upstairs, Lacy laid in bed for a little praying about her doubts and uncertainties. After letting her mind rest, she drifted off to sleep. There was something about her bed at home that made her fall asleep right away—maybe the silk pillowcase or the foam for extra comfort; whatever it was, it made her sleep like a baby.

Chapter Eight

The next morning was a wake-up call for Nathan. He woke up and had to remind himself that he was back at his apartment. He usually woke up before the rest of the guys, so he spent this time praying about what, if anything, he should do to pursue Lacy.

About an hour later, the rest of the guys woke up, and it was time to eat breakfast. They got dressed for the day and headed back to base to get breakfast at the mess hall. As they arrived, the room smelled like eggs, bacon, and much more. There were a few different breakfast choices, including grits, cereal, and fruit. Nathan and his friends sat down at one of the tables and enjoyed all the food they could fit on one plate before the day started.

"This food is actually pretty good," Clyde remarked.

"I know! Having grits for breakfast! I forgot how much the mess hall has changed over the years," JJ said.

"I know. We've been just having cereal at the apartment most days. I guess we are missing out," Martin replied.

"Y'all are right," Nathan said as he took another spoonful of the grits.

They were in the mess hall for about fifteen minutes and then headed to the gym for physical training. The days were usually similar, but the training differed. The current day started with PT, and then they went to the firing range for target practice. Even though Nathan was a corpsman, he still needed to be prepared just like a Marine for any situation.

Nathan and the others' CO, Commanding Officer, entered the room. Time froze as all the people in the room stopped what they were doing to salute their officer.

"At ease," the CO said.

The commanding officer continued. "Before we go to the firing range today, I just wanted to make you aware that I just got informed our battalion will be deployed in the next few weeks." Everyone in the room listened carefully to what their officer was saying. Afghanistan is where they would be deployed, but the specific location was not able to be disclosed. He advised them on preparations, which included getting bills in order, packing bags for deployment, which was pretty easy to do because most of the time they would be in the Marine greenside uniforms, and updating letters for loved ones in case they died overseas.

The CO concluded with, "Okay, let's go to the range."

The whole crew got into the car and headed to the firing range. When they got there, they each got in front of their target and started shooting. They were not allowed to leave until everyone hit the right targets, and their CO was extra strict today since deployment was near.

Meanwhile, Lacy woke up from a very long sleep and snacked on a few of the muffins in the tin that her mom left out. Her mom, dad, and Hannah left a note saying they went Black Friday shopping, and the rest of her family left to go back home. Her brother did not live very far away from the house, but they still wanted to return home. Cody traveled back to college early to get ready for the next week. Lacy never had an interest in shopping, in general, and she would not even think about it on Black Friday of all days. All she wanted to do with the day off was take it easy, and that was exactly what she did. After eating her muffin, she packed up the rest of her clothes and put them neatly back into her suitcase. Every piece of clothing rolled up in its place to make it easier to unpack later. She zipped up the last compartment of the suitcase and placed it upright on the floor. The rest of the day, Lacy spent her time on the couch watching TV.

The last two days had left her exhausted mentally and physically.

Who knows when my family is getting back. So, I have some time alone, Lacy thought. As she watched TV, she tried her hardest to not be consumed with her thoughts about Nathan. She tried to engulf herself into the TV show instead of letting her mind wander, and, for the most part, it worked. Every once in a while, Lacy would get up to get some food or grab something she needed from upstairs. She was there for hours when finally, she heard the turn of the key in the lock.

"Lacy, you still here?" her mom said as she entered the house.

"Yes. I'm on the couch."

"Okay. We just got back."

"How was it?"

"Crazy... but we got a lot of good deals!" her mom replied.

"And you, Dad?"

It had been Micah's first time going Black Friday shopping. "A once in a lifetime experience...but I would never do it again," he replied with a sigh.

"My thoughts exactly," Lacy agreed.

"So, what have you been up to all day?" Micah asked.

"You are looking at it," she said with a chuckle.

"Well, it is much-needed rest for you."

"Yeah. I've enjoyed it."

They talked for a little bit longer. Not once did Nathan come into the conversation. Lacy gave a sigh of relief.

"So, what is your plan for the rest of the night?" Lacy's mom asked.

"I've packed, and I'm going to go to bed soon since my flight is early tomorrow morning."

"Who is taking you again?" her mom said.

"I can," Lacy's dad replied.

"Okay, are you sure, Dad? Because I could just get a cab."

"I insist."

"Okay. Well, I'm off to bed. See you at 1 am."

"Then I better get off to bed after I have some dinner."

"Yeah, after the day you had," Lacy teased.

Lacy went upstairs, got ready for bed, and struggled to get to sleep. She laid in bed for hours, tossing and turning. After three hours of no sleep, she looked at her phone and saw that it was about 9 pm. She had four hours left before she would have to be up. She turned onto her side, closed her eyes, and finally drifted off to sleep. Four hours came quickly, and her alarm went off, letting her know it was time to get up.

Before she got dressed in her comfy traveling clothes, she thought of reasons she could not sleep.

Maybe it was something I ate... but then my stomach didn't hurt. Or maybe it was because something was on my mind even though I was thinking much about it. Or maybe a noise kept me up. The different possibilities swirled in Lacy's head.

However, she did not know that Nathan was up thinking about her and his soon-to-be deployment. He was home from base getting some things in order, and then he chose to spend some time with the guys. They planned to have a guy's night, and he needed that distraction.

"Hey, Nathan, you ready to have some fun?" Clyde asked.

"Yes, let's have a blast! Are we staying in or going out?"

"We are staying in. We are going to have a video game tournament night."

"Sounds good to me. You guys might cream me, though, since I don't play as much."

The guys put the different video games in a stack and then choose five out of the ten to include in the tournament. The first game was a racing game with multiple different places to drive, and you could go against others online or friends. There were 12 different places to travel in the game, and in the end, the top three for all the races would earn gold, silver, and bronze. Each guy picked a character as his driver and a car to steer on the courses.

After everyone picked, they started. JJ started off with the winning streak, beating the rest of the boys on the first five courses. However, he was left in the dust when Clyde came out of nowhere and won the remainder of the courses. The last course consisted of a virtual golf course where they had to drive on the green, trying to avoid the sandpits and other obstacles that could get in their way. Martin got stuck in the water and spent most of the time trying to catch up. Nathan was so close to winning the last game, but halfway through the course, he got stuck in a sandpit and had difficulty escaping it. He ended up finally getting out of it and somehow still landed second place.

At the end of the game, the results were: 1st place to Clyde, 2nd place to JJ, 3rd Place to Martin, and Nathan in dead last. They had enough of that game and moved on to a virtual football game where they picked different players from real football teams and used the controls to make plays. Each captain picked one more person to be on their team, and the game began. As they were playing, Nathan thought of the real football game that he had played just two days earlier. It was the first time that he thought of her the whole night. Before he went down that trail in his mind, he stopped himself and expressed his thanks for such a fun night.

"Thanks for the night, guys. I really needed it."

"Goodnight," JJ and Martin said as they left to go to their rooms.

"Are you thinking about her?" Clyde inquired when it was just the two of them left.

"Well, I wasn't until you said something."

"Uh-uh..." he replied.

"Okay, I will admit I've debated about what to do since we are going to be deployed soon... but I was fully present at our game tournament."

"Just be honest with her and see what she says."

"I know... but it sounds much easier than it actually is."

"No excuses. If you want any relationship, you have to make an effort. Goodnight, bro." "Goodnight." And as Nathan headed to his room, he knew his best friend was right. He had to do something if he wanted anything to happen.

Chapter Nine

Lacy quickly threw on a pair of sweatpants and a T-shirt for the plane ride. She would rather be comfortable than try to look nice when she was sitting for a few hours. After she tied her shoes, she grabbed her suitcase before going downstairs. She headed to the kitchen to get the remainder of the muffins that her mom stashed in the fridge. Her dad was not downstairs yet, and she decided if she did not see him in the next few minutes, she would leave him a note and just take a cab. As she was thinking about it, her dad came into the kitchen.

"Hey, sweetie. Let me just grab something, and I'll be ready to go."

"Okay."

He grabbed an apple and a piece of bread. "Okay, let's go!"

They walked out the door and got into his car. The roads, as she assumed, were packed with others trying to get home after the holiday. By leaving at 1 am, there was enough time to get to the airport before her plane took off at 5 am. It was a good thing because the traffic was more horrendous as they got closer to the airport. It took about two hours to get to the airport in DC when on normal travel days, it would take 30-40 minutes. The radio stayed cranked up loud, and the two of them sang to country music to get through dealing with the traffic for the remainder of the trip. The singing helped because, before long, her dad pulled up in the front of the airport and parked in one of the designated visitor spots for drop-off.

"Sweetie, I hope you have a safe trip back to Kansas. Love you," he said as he hugged her.

"Love you too, Dad."

He walked back to the car and drove away. Lacy took her suitcase and got everything checked in. She then reported to the gate. She would still be there for two more hours until boarding, but she always thought it better to be early than rushing to get there on time. So, with that time, she decided to send a text to Nathan. She hesitated before, but she decided not to wait any longer. Her fingers began typing, and before she sent it, she reviewed it to make sure everything sounded right.

"Hey Nathan. I hope all is well. I just wanted to let you know that I've thought about what I said, and if you give me a few months, I think I will be ready. I've had a lot of different feelings, and I think I want to take this risk. Just know it might take time."

The next two hours, she took glances for a text message back from him, but none appeared. In the meantime, she pulled out the same book she read on the last flight to continue reading while waiting for boarding.

It was the part of the story near the climax, so as she read, the hairs on her arm stood up with chills from the words she read. The airport attendant announced her plane boarding, which snapped her out of the fantasy world she had once again escaped to.

He is probably in training, she thought as her plane started to board.

"Well, I guess I'll see what he says when I get back home," she continued to ponder. She moved to her window seat, got her neck pillow adjusted around her neck, and then began reading her book again. She was interrupted when the flight attendant went over the safety instructions and procedures in case of an emergency. Then she returned to her book, which took her into a completely different world until her plane landed hours later. As the plane's wheels touched the ground, she finished the last page of her book with nothing but a smile across her face. It ended just the right way but also at the same time, not the way she expected it to end.

"Please stay seated until the captain turns off the seat belt sign," she heard over the plane's intercom.

A few minutes later, the flight attendant announced that the seat belt sign had been turned off and that everyone was free to deboard. Lacy went to the baggage claim and, to her amazement, it only took a little bit of time for her suitcase to arrive on the conveyor belt. She was back in Kansas and had one more day off before things would go back to normal. Once she got home, she looked at her phone again, and there were two unread messages.

Hey, sorry, Lacy. I was in training all day. There is something I need to tell you, but I'd rather over the phone. Is now a good time?

"Yes," she replied right away.

He dialed the number and, in less than three rings, he heard her beautiful voice again.

"Hey, Lacy."

"Hi, Nathan."

"It is so nice to hear your voice."

"It is good to hear yours, too. So, what's up?"

"I've been struggling with how to word this... so, I'm just going to come out and say it." Nathan hesitated.

"Okay, go for it!"

"First thing is that you know I would wait like I said before... and the second is that I'm being deployed in a few weeks."

There was a moment of silence as Lacy processed what she had just heard.

"Wow... I didn't expect that. Then I guess my question is, what do we do?" Lacy said.

"I have some of the same questions, and that's what I wanted to talk to you about," Nathan replied.

They went back and forth, talking about their plan for the foreseeable future.

"Okay, well, how will we contact one another? Like

email or letters or Skype?" Lacy wondered.

"All of the above could work, but probably Skype and letters every so often could work."

"Okay, and we just leave this as friendship for now?"

"Don't you think that is best until I get back from deployment?"

"Yes, but also, let's not worry too much if that would change. How long is your deployment?

"Agreed. It will probably be about seven months."

They talked for another hour before Lacy almost fell asleep. They talked about what the deployment could be like and more. She knew what a deployment was like because of James, but this was a bit of a different situation. Lacy wanted to know what was expected of her as a friend and if expectations would be different. In the end, they decided to just write letters to each other whenever they got the chance. So, in the end, no expectation was put on either of them.

"Sorry, Nathan, I'm exhausted. I'm going to have to call it quits."

"Goodnight, Lacy. Good luck tomorrow with getting back to work."

"And good luck with you preparing for deployment."

She got off the phone and, unlike the night before, she fell asleep right away.

Chapter Ten

*T*he next day was not the easiest for Lacy. She not only had to wake up early, but it was difficult to get back into the swing of things after a few days off. As it was a Sunday and the only day she could meet her clients, she listened to a sermon at home, then stopped to get coffee at the local coffee shop before heading to her first appointment with Grant and Angela, the couple who got engaged before Lacy left for Thanksgiving. She met them at the house and talked for a few hours about their plan for the wedding.

"I want to get married in April or May," Angela explained.

"That is a great time to get married. Are you thinking inside or out? You don't want to have it in the fall?"

"I don't want to have to wait that long. I love fall, but I love Grant more. I'm thinking inside... especially because the chance of the rain could be so high."

"Well, I could find a venue that is inside, but bring elements from the outside so it feels like you are outside."

"I really like that idea."

They talked about venues, flowers, the reception, wedding theme or colors, and much more. When they were done, Lacy went to her office and began putting the ideas down on paper. She picked up her colored pencils and sketched out what the wedding would look like. Lacy loved taking the ideas from her clients and making their dreams come true. It was one of her favorite parts of her job. She looked back at her sketch when she finished, but something was still missing. She could not quite grasp what was missing, so she decided to take a break and come back to it later with a refreshed mind.

Lacy glanced at her watch and realized that she only had 30 minutes under her next appointment. This appointment was not a consult but the real thing. She stood up from her desk and looked around for everything that needed to go into her car for the event. Then she walked outside, opened up her trunk, and stashed all the decorations inside. She quickly ran back inside to grab a few more things when her phone rang. "Hello, this is Lacy. What can I do for you?"

"This is the florist. I just wanted to clarify that I'm on my way to drop off the flowers at the venue."

"Awesome! I am on my way!" Lacy said as she turned the key in the ignition and drove off.

"Okay, see you there."

The florist hung up, and then someone else called Lacy. Since she already had her phone in the cup holder, she answered it on the first ring. "Hello, this is Lacy."

"Hi, Lacy! This is the caterer. We are preparing for tonight and will be over there in about 5 hours. I just wanted to double-check the address and also if there are any last-minute needs." "Thank you. I think all the food is good, and my clients have not given me any new updates. The address is 3 Tulip Lane, and once you get there, it is the house on the left."

"Great, then I will see you at 5 pm."

Lacy got off the phone. She only had about 10 minutes before she arrived at the venue. She turned onto the long driveway and, a half-mile later, she arrived. She parked her car closest to the venue and tripped over the carpet under her seat before stepping out of her car. Luckily, she caught herself before falling face-first onto the pavement. She walked up the sidewalk to the door and rang the doorbell. In just a few minutes, the door opened, and Lacy was greeted by her client, Frank.

"Hi, Lacy. Thank you for coming. I can't wait to see how you are going to transform the place!"

"I am so excited to help you!"

"My wife is going to love this anniversary party. She loves surprises! If you need any help, let me know!"

"I will. Thank you."

After talking to Frank, Lacy walked herself over to the barn where the event would occur in just the next few hours. She opened the barn door just as the flower delivery van came up the driveway. The two employees walked out of the van and headed towards Lacy. "Hi, you must be Lacy," one of the employees said. "We have the flowers in the van and also the arch that you requested."

"Thank you so much! You can just put the flowers in the barn, and I will take it from there."

"Okay. We are happy to help."

They grabbed some of the flowers and then went back for more. In total, they had to make six trips from the car to the barn before the van was empty. There were about six different flowers, such as amaryllis, sweet peas, camellias, carnations, roses, and tulips. The florists double-checked that she had everything she needed and then walked back to the van to leave. She had five hours to turn the barn from ordinary to a winter wonderland. She loved this job so much because she took ordinary places and turned them into dreamlands.

Lacy walked into the barn and closed her eyes to make the sketch once again come to life. She grabbed the chairs leaning against the side of the barn and began to place them in four different rows on each side. Lacy would be on her own for a few hours before her two employees would come to help with the rest of the decorations. Usually, her two employees divided and conquered working on events if they happened to take place on the same day; otherwise, they would all work together at the event space. Lacy was the boss, but she saw her other employees as equal to her and eventually wanted to give them the freedom to do their own designs. In the meantime, Lacy finished placing the last chair right in its place and then moved to get the flowers. Lacy grabbed the sweet peas and camellias to drape on the chairs. The client's wife loved white and pink, so Lacy wanted to incorporate her favorite colors into the venue's design. She took each flower, intertwined the two flowers together, and loosely placed them using pins on the back of each chair. It took about an hour or so for her to finish, and then she moved on to decorating the arch with the same kind of flowers.

"Excuse me," a mysterious individual said from outside the barn.

Lacy did not even think twice. She thought it was probably the husband coming to see how it was going, so she simply said, "Yes, come in."

"It looks really nice," the mysterious masculine voice commented.

Lacy had not looked up, but the voice sounded so familiar. After moving the arch to the front of the barn, she looked up to see someone she never thought she would see again so soon.

Nathan stood in front of her holding back the desire to run towards her and give her a great big hug.

"What are you doing here?" she said in shock without being able to move.

"I know now that I leave in a week or so, and I couldn't leave without saying goodbye to you one last time."

She still stood in shock for a few minutes, not able

to say a word.

"Are you okay? Maybe I didn't think this through enough. We did just see each other a few days ago," Nathan said, regretting his decision. He had called Lacy's office and spoke to one of her employees about her current location. Her employees knew when Lacy texted them that she had met Nathan, so they entrusted him with knowing her location.

"Sorry, I just wasn't expecting this. I don't know what to say."

"Well, how about while you think about that, I can help you with decorating."

"Yes, that would work. Hold on... before we do... it is really great to see you."

He took this chance to walk closer to her and put his face close to hers. In the unexpected moment, Nathan drew closer, and before Lacy could step back, he put his lips on hers. The kiss only lasted for a moment before Nathan realized how the kiss could make things even more complicated.

"I am sorry."

"No, you don't have to be sorry."

"I just keep on acting on impulse, and I couldn't imagine not leaving without kissing you."

"I'm glad that you acted on your impulse," Lacy said with a quick smile on her face, although she was confused and still in shock.

"Okay, well, I can only be here for a little time, and

then I have to take my flight back to Virginia."

"Well, let's just enjoy the time we have."

"Agreed."

"So, you ready for me to put you to work?"

"Yes. Tell me what you need."

"I'm going to decorate the arch with these flowers. Can you hang up these lights from the ceiling? The ladder is right there in front of you, and here is what I want it to look like. Can you do that?" Lacy said as she showed him her sketches. Instead of hanging the lights completely down like her last event, she had tea lights in different size glasses to hang from the ceiling.

"I got it covered. Don't you worry," Nathan teased.

Lacy worked on putting the roses, camellias, and carnations alternatively on the arch. In the end, she wanted the whole place to feel like a winter wonderland, and the arch would put the finishing touches on the place. Lacy intertwined the three different flowers together in the pattern of red, white, and pink. It would not be an exact pattern because Lacy always liked to make it look real and not perfect. Another thirty minutes went by as she finished placing the last flowers on the arch.

"Hey, I'm finished," Nathan announced. "I just have an hour left until I have to leave. Could we take a short break and talk?"

"Yeah, but it will have to be quick because I still have upstairs to finish."

"I was hoping you were going to say that because I brought some lunch already."

"Look at you thinking ahead." Lacy loved teasing him.

He grabbed some sandwiches and ice cream from the cooler he had in his rental car.

"So, quick question. Did you really just get a rental car for a few hours?"

"Yes. I could have gotten a cab or something, but I wanted to have control to get places."

"So, how were you able to have leave when your deployment is so soon?"

"Don't worry about that. Just know they let me come."

"Okay...Okay, I won't ask anymore then."

The two talked for a half-hour about life, and they talked more about Nathan's deployment with details they did not discuss the night before.

"So, this might be awkward asking, but what happens because of this kiss?" Nathan brought up the elephant in the room.

"I think like we said before, we just see what happens and get to know each other better while you're on deployment."

"So, the kiss doesn't change anything?"

"Of course, it does! But I still need more time to get to know you before we go for this relationship. We've only known each other a few days, and I don't want to rush anything when there is still so much to know. And I also don't want to get into something if I am not ready to. Do you understand?"

"Yes. Okay, I guess that is the best option." He was a little disappointed, but he did see why Lacy felt that way.

Nathan looked at the time and saw that it was time to go. It seemed that he was only there for a few minutes, and he already had to turn around to go back home.

Is this how it will feel to have a long-distance relationship? he thought.

"Lacy, unfortunately, I have to go... I really don't want to."

"You have to... I know that. Just be safe over there, you hear me?" Lacy said with a concerned tone.

"I'll do my best!"

Before Nathan got back into the car, he took Lacy in his arms and passionately kissed her. He thought about how he would not see her for seven months, and the impulse took over once again. This time the kiss lingered a little longer than before. He was about to go when Lacy grabbed his hand and hugged him one last time.

"I mean it. Stay safe!"

"Okay. Bye."

And just like that, he was out of her life again, driving off with the possibility that he would never return. It became more surreal to her that he might die overseas. She tried to replace the scenarios going through her head so that fear would not take over her thoughts, but it would not be easy. She watched his car as he drove away and only hoped that he would return to her after the next seven months.

Chapter Eleven

Once the car was no longer in the distance, Lacy went back to work by putting down a white aisle runner in the barn before taking the rest of the red, white, and pink roses left to sprinkle on the aisle. Then she climbed the stairs up to the loft. In the loft, six round tables were already set up just where they needed to be. Lacy walked back down the stairs and to her car to get the linens and the boxes of centerpiece decorations out of her trunk. While she was juggling the boxes in her hands, her two employees came to help her. They walked up to the loft and set each table the same way with a white linen tablecloth and a crystal vase centerpiece. Then Lacy took the tulips and put a dozen of them in each vase. The tulips ranged from light pinks, whites, and another shade of darker pink. She put the last finishing touches on upstairs by putting pictures of the lovely couple around the room. The photos were little snapshots of memories the couple had from when they first met all the way to a picture from a few weeks prior. Lacy's phone was ringing again, and she figured it was the caterers.

"Hello, this is Lacy. How can I help you?"

"This is the caterer. We just arrived with the food."

"Awesome. I will be right down."

Lacy took one last glance to make sure all the decorations worked with the setting and then ran down the stairs and out of the barn. The caterers arrived in a white van, and some of the workers hopped out of the back of the van.

"Hi, Lacy. It is great to see you again!"

"Yes, I always love your food. I am glad for our partnership."

"Okay, well, show us where you want everything placed."

"Follow me."

Lacy directed all of them to the loft, where two rectangle tables were set up, ready for all the food to sit on. The caterers grabbed as much as they could and placed it on the tables with the little heaters underneath to keep it warm for a few hours for the guests. Once everything was set and ready, it was time for the event to begin. Lacy walked out of the barn and moved her car to hide it from anyone who could see it. If she really wanted it to be a surprise, then she had to make sure that nothing could give away what was happening. Her client's wife would be home any minute, and then the night would finally begin. Lacy was so fixated on everything being done that she did not have a moment to think about what happened between her and Nathan. She did not fully process what it meant, and until this event finished, she would push it aside in her mind. Her client came out to the barn as she closed up the door. It would be a surprise for both of them in some ways.

"Everything ready!" he said, smiling from ear to ear.

"Yes! You're going to have to wait until your wife comes to see the rest, though." "Alright. I guess I will. She just texted me, and she should be home in 2 minutes."

Just as he was saying that, his wife drove up and walked in the door.

"Honey, I'm home."

Lacy slipped out the back door and back to the barn. From now on, she would work the rest of the time behind the scenes, not to be seen.

"Hey, honey. Happy Anniversary," the man said.

"Happy Anniversary to you, too," she said, leaning in to give him a peck on the lips.

"So, I thought that we could have a nice night in and go for a walk," her husband commented.

"Sounds good to me, honey. Let me just change into something different than my scrubs."

When she finished changing her clothes, the couple walked out to the brisk outside air and moved towards the barn. Lacy requested from the very beginning that the guests would arrive after the wife and her husband were in the barn. They walked through the area where the horses were because his wife always loved to pet the horses. It was also a great distraction so that the guests could come into the barn and sit down without his wife knowing. His wife stopped to brush her horse for a little bit. As she brushed, she felt the coarse knots in the horse's mane and slowly detangled each one with the brush. She brushed every last tangle out before putting the brush down and going to the next horse. Once everyone arrived, Lacy gave the okay for her client to come.

"Ready to go!" Lacy texted.

"On the way."

"They are on the way!" Lacy exclaimed to the guests.

The couple walked from the horse barn through a small hallway to the front of the barn. Everyone in the barn was absolutely silent, and then the barn door opened. When his wife opened the door, to her amazement, there was a full house of people looking up at her as she was escorted by her husband down the aisle. Both of their eyes lit up at the winter wonderland of the barn, and they were speechless. He never let go of his wife's hand. Lacy always anticipated doing an event for a couple or wedding because she was a romantic at heart, and seeing the love in their eyes just melted her heart every time.

"What are we doing here?" the wife asked.

"Well, honey, I thought that we could renew our vows."

"You surprised me. That doesn't happen often," she whispered as they walked down the aisle. They renewed their vows, and it brought memories back. Then all the guests followed the couple up to the loft, and each sat down at their assigned seat. The couple was now married for 40 years, and they shared good and difficult memories during dinner time. A dance floor was non-existent, but the couple somehow found a little space in the loft to move around. After being married for 40 years, they did not need music to dance.

Lacy finished up with one last thing, and then she went home. The day was long, and she needed a nice rest before cleaning up everything the next day.

In the meantime, Nathan arrived back at the airport in Virginia and headed home. The whole time he was on the plane, his mind could not let go of the moment he shared with Lacy. It made it even harder for him to leave her, knowing that he would have her as his wife one day. He could get ahead of himself with his thoughts, but deep inside, he knew that the Lord put her in his life for this purpose. He had never had a feeling like this before and could not imagine having it with anyone else. He drifted off to sleep with the thought that no matter how long it took, he and Lacy would be married someday. Usually, he would think of nothing but his deployment this close to it, but this time his thoughts wandered elsewhere.

Chapter Twelve

A week passed, and it was time for Nathan and the boys to leave for deployment. They rushed out of bed to get ready. Usually, they would be the first ones there, but for some reason, their alarm did not go off, and they woke up 20 minutes later than usual.

"Hey, Nathan, it's time to go," Clyde said, knocking on his bedroom door.

"Coming!" Nathan replied.

"We need to get to base so we can go with our whole battalion to the airport," Clyde said, running around the apartment to make sure everyone was getting ready.

"Let's go! I'm ready!" Nathan said as he ran downstairs to the front door.

All the boys ran out of the house and to the car. JJ got in the driver's seat, and they were off. They got to the base and joined the rest of their battalion just as the bus was being loaded up. The whole battalion got on the bus a few people at a time, and then the bus driver took the highway to the airport. Nathan and his friends sat together. His friends started to talk about the deployment, while Nathan kept to himself. They could see that he was in another world. Clyde knew that he could let Nathan daydream or could ask Nathan what he was thinking about. He decided to ask Nathan a few questions and then leave him alone the rest of the ride.

"How did it go? You haven't told me the latest update," Clyde inquired.

"Well, yes…I went to Kansas, and I surprised her when she was getting ready for one of her events. It is amazing how she transforms something so ordinary into something extraordinary. Anyways, I surprised her…and well, I kissed her. It made things a little awkward…and then I helped her with putting up lights in the barn… and lastly, I brought lunch, and we ate outside of the barn. We talked about what would happen, and then before leaving, I kissed her again. I was about to leave, and she grabbed my arm to give me a long hug and remind me to stay safe. I know she is going to be my wife someday…but I still feel that she is not sure if she can do this life again." He said this really jumbled and fast.

"Just give it time. Think about if you were in her situation. How would you feel about dating and possibly something more with someone in the military after such a tragedy?" Clyde wanted Nathan to think about how she would feel and, maybe then, he would understand why she was unsure about what to call their relationship.

"Wow, when did you get good at giving relationship

advice?" Nathan said sarcastically.

"Guess it just comes naturally."

The other boys, JJ and Martin, eavesdropped on the conversation and interrupted.

"Wow, man, so proud of you," JJ said.

"So y'all are just friends even after what happened?" Martin questioned.

"Well, first, thanks for listening. She said for now to be just friends, and that is what I was just telling Clyde. I think that she is scared to move on to anything more, but maybe these next months will change that."

JJ eagerly asked another question. "Was she surprised?"

"Yes, she was speechless for a few moments, and she just stood there. I wanted to wrap my arms around her and kiss her, but at first, I ignored the impulse... until I didn't."

The conversation finished just in time for them to arrive at the airport. The whole battalion walked together to the plane that would take them across the seas to their assignment for the next seven months. Nathan took one last look at American soil before he boarded the plane.

~

Meanwhile, Lacy got up early so that she could

pray for Nathan and his time on deployment. When she got a second to breathe, Lacy finally replayed the last week in her thoughts. Her thoughts went all over the place.

"I've never thought I would feel this way before, and at the same time, I'm still confused and anxious about being in a relationship with another service member. But I also want to take the risk, but can I really go through that again?"

Her thoughts were like a ping pong game going back and forth with what decision to make. She realized the only way to get a true answer or peace from the situation was by praying about it.

Hey God. You have given me such a great life, and you've helped me through so many challenges.

Lord, I ask for wisdom in this moment to listen to you and make the right decision, whether Nathan is supposed to stay in my life or if I am feeling these emotions, but they don't mean anything. Lord, you know if I am supposed to find another love with Nathan or someone else. Lord, I ask that my eyes and ears are open to you telling and guiding me to what is according to your plan. Lord, I also just pray for Nathan again and that you watch over him and his fellow Marines as they go on deployment. I pray that they know they can trust and surrender everything to you. Lord, help me to give all my anxiety over to you and let you give me peace that can only come from you.

Lacy finished her prayer with an amen and then drifted off to sleep for a few more hours. When she woke up, she realized that it was Sunday morning, which meant she needed to get ready for church. She dressed in black pants and a maroon shirt paired with a white cardigan. She held on to her heavier coat and took it to the car if she needed it in church or after church, depending on if the weather changed.

Most Sunday mornings, Lacy headed to church and then afterward would take the rest of the day off to go hiking or just stay at home. It was her time to spend in nature and when she felt the closest to God in His presence. Of course, during football season, that would not happen, but any other time, she would take the opportunity to go hiking whenever she got the chance. During football season, she would be sitting on the couch watching as many games as possible.

On this particular day, the weather was too cold to go hiking. Instead, after church, she went home and took a long winter's nap. While she was sleeping, the memory of her fiancé James filled her dreams:

~ About 8 years before ~

*J*ames Townson walked across the campus grass with a smile across his face. He loved to enjoy the nice spring weather. He knew that he would be in boot camp for the Navy a year later and, soon after that, probably deployed. As he enjoyed the weather, he noticed someone sitting under a tree with a book in her hand. At first, he just stared and, after a minute or so, the girl looked up at him, but then she looked back down. James took that glance from her as an opportunity and walked over to her.

"Hi, I'm James."

She looked up to see a very handsome man, 6'2", brown eyes, with tanned skin and dark brown short hair staring at her from three feet away. The first thing she noticed was his smile, a smile that could be worth a million bucks. His smile was contagious, and as much as she tried to hide it, it made her smile, too. "Hi, I'm Lacy." She honestly wanted nothing to do with him because he was interrupting her studying.

"I know this might be weird, but I noticed you, and I wanted to see if you wanted to go out sometime."

"Um...well, I was not expecting that. Here is the deal; if you can help me study for an hour, then I will go on a date with you." She thought it would make him leave, but her idea backfired.

"That is an easy deal. I'm in!" James said. He would do anything to take her on a date.

They spent the next hour studying—actually studying—and even in that time, Lacy could see that he had a good character. He helped her memorize different capitals for geography class. He then also spent a little bit of time helping her study math. She thought, *why wouldn't I say yes?*

The hour ended, and he said, "Okay, so a deal is a deal. I will see you in an hour?" He walked away so that she had no chance to back out of the date.

"Yes, you win. See you in an hour," she said, excited but also a little annoyed.

An hour later, James showed up in jeans and a nice navy-blue pullover sweater. Lacy came out of her dorm building with a similar outfit to his, except that she had blue jeans paired with a gray three-quarter zipped sweater. She laughed as she realized they were almost dressed the same. She walked over to him, and he waved as he saw her coming closer.

"You look beautiful!" he said, not realizing yet that they were sort of matching.

"You don't look so bad yourself." Lacy never flirted, but with this man, it seemed so easy.

"Should we go?" he said, starting to replace confidence with nervousness.

"Where are we going?" she inquired.

"I thought that we would go to this new restaurant that I've wanted to try out."

"You mean the new pizza place?" she asked, barely able to contain her excitement about trying the new place.

"Yes!"

"Absolutely! I've wanted to try that out for a while now."

~

*T*he memories transported her back to the emotions she felt those years ago when the stranger James Townson walked into her life. Lacy woke up from her nap with tears in her eyes and a smile on her face. The dream was real and such a bittersweet moment looking back at it. However, God showed her through the memory that the answer was clear. She needed to give Nathan a chance at love, just like she did for James all those years ago.

Chapter Thirteen

Nathan and the battalion hit the ground almost a day later. Once his boots hit the ground, he knew that he could not be distracted by his thoughts. He let them go and focused on the task at hand. The next day they would really get to work. He knew there would not be much free time, so he took the time to write his first letter to Lacy. It would be his last time to think about her before focusing one hundred percent on his mission.

Dear Lacy,

I know that it has only been a few days but I thought I would write this before things get crazy over here. I really enjoyed the time we got to spend together in Kansas. I just arrived at the base and the real work starts tomorrow. I know that there are a lot of things you need to think about but I'm going to just express how I feel to you clearly. I think that you are very special and that I couldn't imagine not getting to know you better. I can really see a future with you and I don't want that to scare you. I want to be here to comfort you when you're sad and laugh with you. I really care about you. We may not be able to talk all the time while I'm over here, but know even without communicating that I am thinking about you.

Sincerely,

Nathan

It would take about 14 days or more for the mail to arrive, and, in the meantime, he would not have time to think about waiting on a letter. He put the pen down and fell asleep knowing life was about to be extremely different once again.

Chapter Fourteen

While Nathan was on deployment, his special assignment left no time for Skyping Lacy, and there was no access to email. They could only rely on letters, and he never received one back after he sent his four months ago. He thought the worst. *She decided I wasn't worth giving a chance.* This worst-case scenario went through his head over and over again in the last few months. At the same time, he tried not to think about it. It seemed like there was never a break. Day after day, more Marines suffered both minor and major injuries. He was busy trying to save their lives, which did not leave much time for anything else. He might have seen her as the love of his life, but he needed to help his fellow Marines so that they could also get back to their loved ones. Nothing would get in his way to save as many lives as he could.

Lacy thought the same kind of thoughts as Nathan. She never got the letter from Nathan, and after she sent him her letter, she never got one back. They thought that they would be communicating throughout the seven months, but it turned out that they had already lost four months of communication.

It was a sunny, chilly day in April when Lacy returned from another event and checked her mailbox. After not hearing from Nathan in four months, she had become more worried that something terrible had happened. She tried not to think about it, but the thought always came back to her. She had almost given up hope that a letter would come, but when she checked, to her amazement, she finally saw a letter addressed to her from Nathan among the other letters and bills in the mailbox.

"Oh, my gosh! Whew!" Lacy said out loud, relieved.

She ripped open the envelope and opened the letter. It was refreshing to read the note and know that he was still okay. However, as she read the letter, she saw in the right top corner that the date said the letter was written in December. It still gave her peace, but she wondered why neither of their letters made it to each other. She read the letter over again and again. She knew what it said, but when she was reading it, it made her feel that he was right there with her. She pulled out a new sheet of paper and began writing the same letter she had written before.

If I got his letter, maybe he would get my letter too, she thought.

Chapter Fifteen

Nathan was back at the base in Afghanistan, and for the first time in a while, his team got some free time. The guy in charge of getting the mail came into Nathan's bunk.

"Nathan! You got some mail!"

He heard that, and his face immediately perked up as if he were a kid getting candy at the candy store. One of the men handed the envelope to him. He saw who it was from and was overjoyed. Then as fast as he could, he used his pocketknife to rip open the letter.

He read the letter from Lacy, holding on to every word:

Dear Nathan,

I'm at home and thinking about a million things, so you know what I thought I should do... take a nap. During my nap God gave me the answer that I've been praying for. I have to tell you and I'm not going to wait until you get back. To be honest, I've told you how scared I am to give you a chance after what happened with James. However, I woke up with this peace that I can be with you and not worry about you never coming back from war. I want to get to know you more and not just as friends. I want to take this chance and I for the

first time in a long time can see a future with someone...
someone like you. I'm praying for you and your whole
battalion to be safe and come home safely.

Sincerely,

Lacy

Nathan did not get emotional much, but after reading her letter, he wished that he could just go run into her arms. He could not imagine how she felt with him being away, especially without being able to contact him. He grabbed a pen and began writing right away. There was something about writing her that felt so comforting.

Dear Lacy,

When I got your letter it made me feel that you were right here. It has been a tough four months over here. Nothing you want to hear about. I will say that there are many Marines that I've had to help with over here. Unfortunately, some of the men in my battalion lost their lives on a mission. Please pray for their friends and family. I know I am doing all I can to save their lives, but sometimes I wish I could do more. I've also had the opportunity to meet some great guys in another battalion working with mine and assisted in helping one of the Marines get to better health so he could return to his family. He had to go back to the US, but he is lucky that he survived. Anyways, when I read what you said it made me excited and ready to jump into your arms in a few months. I hope that you are doing okay and what you wrote four months ago is still true. You are such a special person and I'm sorry that we've lost this time to talk. I think it has grown my desire to want to get to know you more. It's April so I bet that you have events lined up back-to-back with weddings scheduled. Remember to make time for yourself. I've been praying about us and I also feel that God has told me how we are to pursue this relationship. See you in a few months!

Love, Nathan.

He signed the letter, folded it up, and addressed the envelope. Then he rushed to get the letter in the mail.

Then Nathan spent some time playing football with the boys. It took him back to the Thanksgiving football game. It seemed like when he got the chance to think that everything reminded him of Lacy. It made him not only miss her but also think of his parents. He started to feel homesick, and he still had three months left to go. The boys played a game up to 30 and then took the rest of the night to get some sleep before going on another assignment the next day.

Chapter Sixteen

A song played on Lacy's cell phone, and she turned over in her bed to hit the snooze button. However, the alarm on her phone had done its job. She woke up, and no matter what she tried to do, her body was wide awake. Lacy stared at the ceiling, dreading to get up for work pretty much every morning. She loved her job. However, waking up early, even routinely, was not the easiest thing for her to do. She could feel her eyes closing and opening for the next hour as she lay in bed, wishing she could spend the rest of the day cuddled up in her covers.

She decided the night before that she would be moving back to Virginia, and the reality hit her. She thought she would have to start all over in Virginia while her business continued to expand in Kansas. She thought of all the logistics, but in the end, that did not matter. She missed being around her family, and she knew it was time to return to the place that always had a place in her heart. Before James died, she thought she would always stay in Virginia, but she ran away from her circumstances instead. Lacy knew that moving on also meant that she was ready to move back to where her heart always belonged.

After putting off getting ready for an hour, Lacy finally put her feet on the floor and got dressed for the day. Now that she had made her decision, she needed to talk with her employers about what it would look like, and she also needed to tell her parents. As she pondered the steps she needed to make for moving back home, her phone rang three times.

"Hi. Good morning, Rose. Is something up?" Lacy answered with a muffled voice on the phone. "You are late. You are never late," Rose exclaimed.

"Sorry. I've had a hard time getting up. I'll be in the office in fifteen minutes. There isn't a rush, is there?"

"No. Just a little worried since you are usually always here early," Rose said with a hint of concern.

"When I do get there, we need to talk about something important," Lacy acknowledged. "Got it, boss."

Lacy put on a maroon skirt and a white blouse. She did not have much time to do her hair, so she threw it into a nice bun and called it a day. She walked out the door, hopped into her car, and headed to the office. She walked in the door to be greeted by a cheerful Rose.

"Morning, boss," Rose said.

"Morning," Lacy replied, still trying to wake up without her morning coffee.

"Doing better now?"

"Yes. I'm getting there," Lacy said between yawns.

"You look tired," Rose exclaimed.

"I didn't get the best sleep last night."

"I'm sorry. Well, it's good that we don't have any events today. We only have to work on sketches."

"I know... that is almost a miracle at this time of the year." Lacy sighed with relief.

"So, Lacy, what did you want to talk to me about?"

"Yes, um, well, I need to talk to Susan, too," Lacy said just as Susan walked into the room.

"I'm here, boss," Susan exclaimed as she walked closer to them.

"Okay, you're the first to hear this. I've been thinking and praying about this a lot, and I am going to be moving in the next few months. I know you probably have a lot of questions, but let me say it all first. I've always seen this place as temporary. Y'all work so hard, and I know that my leaving could change things, but I think that things could even get better. I'm not moving my company but expanding it. Rose and Susan, I want y'all to take over my event company here, and I will start it in Virginia. I know it might be something you need to think about, but y'all worked with me for years, and you are ready to do your own thing. I need to move back home, and I know I'm leaving my company here in good hands."

Rose was in shock. It took her a moment to process before asking a question, "When exactly will you be moving?"

"I am trying to move within the next three months, but it could be more, and it could be less. If I can figure out a place to live, then it could be sooner than later. My parents told me that people have already heard about my event business in Virginia, so by the time I get there, I might already have some clients lined up."

"What if they want you and not us?" Susan asked with concern.

"You have nothing to worry about. I'm going to talk to some of my recurring clients and let them know that y'all are more than capable of doing this together...and if they don't feel the same way, please don't take it personally."

"Wow, this is a shock," Susan commented once she was able to process it.

"I know, and I'm sorry for it being sudden. We will work on other details, but let's just enjoy our time off and work on ideas for this next event."

"Okay, Susan, we can do this! It will be fun!" Rose said.

"That's the spirit."

Lacy and her team worked on the event that they would be doing in the next month. They talked about everything they needed for the event, and each of them started working on possible sketches to share with the clients the next day. The specific event was for a high school graduation. The soon-to-be graduate was picky, and therefore, they wanted to have multiple ideas to share with her. They all had different perspectives, and sharing ideas helped them to compose something with each idea incorporated.

Before leaving for the office that day, the girls stopped Lacy. "We are going to miss you."

"I will miss working with y'all too! You sure you just don't want to move with me?"

"We can't," said Rose.

"I know. I was just kidding. Just like Virginia is my home... Kansas is where you belong... plus that would be too much for your families to pick up and move."

"Exactly."

"Well, goodnight. I will meet you at our soon-to-be graduate's house tomorrow around 11 am."

"See you tomorrow, boss."

Then Lacy crashed the minute she got home. It was only 6 pm, but she was exhausted. She wondered if she could be sick because she was never this tired. She took a nap and woke up at 8 pm to her phone ringing. She usually forgot to look at the caller ID, but this time, she read that it was her mom on the other end of the line. *Just in time*, she thought.

"Hi, Mom!"

"Hi, I just wanted to check in on you! I haven't heard from you other than a few texts here and there."

"I've been really busy, but I was actually just about to call you."

"Oh? Why?"

"I have something important I want to tell you."

"You and Nathan are dating?" Her mom said, trying not to get over-excited.

"No, not yet… but actually, I did get a letter finally from him a few weeks ago."

"Oh, good. So, then what?"

"I've been thinking about this for a while… I thought that it would be later, like a few years from now, but I changed my mind. I want to move back to Virginia, and I think I am ready for the memories that come with moving back." Lacy shared with her mom as her mom listened earnestly.

"Are you sure?"

"Yes… I know it won't be the easiest, especially walking around and remembering all the times with James there, but I need to come back close to home."

"Well, then, in that case! YES! Do you know how long I've waited to have you back closer to us!"

"I have, and I'm sorry that I ran away after James' death. That is when I should've stayed the closest."

"It's okay. I understand why you did."

Then her dad must have heard the news because you could hear him cheering in the background.

"Dad?"

"Yes. Oh, I can't wait!"

"It will be at least a few months. I hope you know that even though I'm moving back, I'm not going to be living with y'all…maybe temporary but not forever."

"Yes, we understand. We will just be glad to have you back," Mom said.

"And you know who else will be happy to have you closer?" her dad teased.

"Let me guess...Nathan," Lacy sassed back.

"Yes. Did this decision have anything to do with him?" Her dad continued to chime into the conversation.

"Honestly, not really. I just felt like it was time, and I was ready."

"Good. Well, we love you and cannot wait to have you here," her mom and dad both said as they started to hang up the phone.

"Okay, love you both," Lacy said right before the call dropped.

The only person left to tell was Nathan, but she didn't even know if she could get a hold of him before he came back.

Chapter Seventeen

Another three weeks went by, and to Lacy, it felt like a lifetime. Lacy anxiously awaited to hear from Nathan. She was starting to get concerned that he might be injured or worse. Just as she started to lose hope, she saw a letter tucked between a mound of bills. With all her might, she tore open the envelope and opened the letter. She read the letter, cherishing every word as tears began to flow down her face. She stopped in the middle of reading to stop and pray for the families that would never get to see their family members again. She could sympathize with each family, and hearing the devastating news brought even more tears. She spent time praying over the letter and the rest of the battalion before she opened up her journal, tore out a piece, and began writing.

Dear Nathan,

You don't know how great it is to know that you are okay. To be honest I started to think that something happened or that you got injured. I am so glad to hear from you! I'm sorry for those men that you lost. I can't imagine how you have to deal with death every day. I know that the men are grateful to have you and that even if you are the last one they see they are dying knowing someone cares. I am praying for you, your battalion, and all the families affected. I'm glad that you are able to also enjoy and find the light in such a dark place. I miss you and can't wait to hold you in my arms. There is something you should know. Do you remember how we talked about me moving back...well, I've made a decision to move back to Virginia in about a month. I chose this for me. I am ready to live back where my home has always been. It's just a bonus that we won't have to be long distance once you return.

See you soon,

Lacy

Lacy took the letter and tucked it as neatly as she could in the envelope. She grabbed a few pieces of tape and secured the envelope. Before attaching the stamp on the front side, she put her lips on the envelope and sealed it with a kiss. Then she walked out to the mailbox and put the letter once again in the hands of the Postal Service. She hoped the letter would reach Nathan before he left Afghanistan.

However, Nathan would never get the letter. It would not arrive at his battalion because the letter was lost somewhere on its journey to Nathan. Nathan figured Lacy did not write back, and Lacy figured that something horrible must have happened once again. For the rest of his deployment, they had no communication for the second time in the long seven months apart from each other.

As Lacy finished walking back from the mailbox, Nathan and the battalion were headed out on a mission in Afghanistan. They went into a town that was destroyed by previous firefights and bombings. Some of the Marines got a tip that there was a bomb in the town, and they used their bomb-sniffing dog, Leo, to check out exactly what they were dealing with. Even though Nathan was a corpsman, he did the same things as the rest of the battalion, unless one of his own got hurt. In this particular mission, JJ got caught up in a heavy ambush of gunshots and could not escape before getting shot. Nathan grabbed JJ by the back of his uniform as the blood flowed down JJ's arm and over the rest of his uniform. Nathan knew from the waterfall of blood coming down JJ's arm that the bullet struck an artery. If he did not stop the bleeding in the next couple of minutes, there would be no chance that he would live. To stop the bleeding temporarily, he found what he could to make a tourniquet. Just as he was helping JJ, another member from the battalion got shot in the head. The man was not as lucky and immediately died from the bullet's impact going right through his brain. Shots went back and forth, and gunfire sounds echoed. Whenever Nathan thought there was more than he could handle, he would say a quick prayer. This time it meant more because the person he was trying to save was not just a teammate but a close friend.

God, please watch over JJ that he will be okay and

make it through and be able to return home safely and heal quickly. I pray for the members who made the ultimate sacrifice today. Lord, help me and be with me the rest of the day. Lord, I ask that you watch over our battalion each day as we go out to the unknown and deal with the unexpected. Amen.

After his prayer, the helicopter spun down to pick up JJ along with the others injured. Just as soon as they came, they disappeared into the smoke-filled sky. The next few hours, the gunfire died down, and the rest of the team regrouped. In the next few weeks, while JJ was shipped back to the United States and taken to be evaluated at the hospital near DC, the battalion continued to search towns for bombs. The next two months consisted of similar missions. They lost more men and women, and it began to hit Nathan harder each time. One of the men stepped on an IED while searching a town and unfortunately did not make it. Yet another was lucky for being at the same place and only suffering hearing loss from the blast. However, before long, it was time for the whole battalion, what was left of it, to travel home and finally get some peace and renewed family time.

Chapter Eighteen

ost of the battalion spent the 20-hour flight getting some much-needed sleep. As the plane touched down and the wheels hit the runway, everyone was excited to see their friends or family members. Nathan did not plan to be greeted by any family or friends. He knew that sometimes his parents would come, but he did not expect them to come this time around. His parents would come after his first few deployments, but it was more of a rare occasion as he got older. His parents tried their best to go and visit, but lately, their workload and the distance from him made it nearly impossible. His parents both worked at a senior level in their company, which meant that many people relied on them to be available at all times. He saw others go up to their spouses and embrace them. It made him think of Lacy, which led to an impulsive decision to go to Kansas to see her. He made a lot of impulsive decisions recently, but luckily nothing too risky.

Meanwhile, Lacy arrived at the DC airport from Kansas. Within the last month, she moved and shipped her boxes to a new rented townhouse. This last trip was just for the remainder of her things, and now she was officially a resident of Virginia again. She pushed through the crowds and saw military service members embracing one another at the different gates. She wondered if Nathan was on his way home and if, somehow, she would run into him before exiting the airport.

Before she could find out, she saw someone that looked like him in the distance. His back was turned toward her, so she was unsure if it was Nathan or someone who looked similar to him. She looked away and headed closer to the airport exit when she noticed another man with Nathan's same features and uniform. She was confused if she saw Nathan or if someone was playing a practical joke on her. She wanted to run up to one of the men, but she could not take the embarrassment if one or both of them ended up not being Nathan. Lacy, confused, began to think about the next best action to take. Before she could think of what to do next, the man in her view glanced in her direction before returning to his conversation. She was unsure before but staring into those piercing green eyes took her breath away, just like the first time she opened the door to the most handsome stranger she had ever seen. She had not experienced this feeling in so long, but instead of being stuck in place, this time she ran to him as fast as she could. The minute her feet got off the ground, it felt like she was flying. When she got close enough, she put her hands over his eyes to surprise him. Her hands shook as she said, "Well, fancy running into you here, my handsome man."

The minute he heard her voice, he turned around and wrapped her in his arms. She felt at home in his arms. He put his lips on hers and gave her a kiss that made up for the seven long months apart, a passionate kiss fit for the movies that expressed without any words how much they missed each other. After the kiss, the conversation started to flow as if it had never stopped.

"I thought you were in Kansas. I was about to get a ticket!" Nathan exclaimed.

"I sent you a letter...you never got it?" Lacy questioned.

"No..."

"Oh, well, I moved back to Virginia, and I just got here from Kansas one last time."

"Seriously... you are playing with me," Nathan teased.

"I'm serious," Lacy said with such a straight face that he knew she was telling the truth. He was so excited that he picked her up off the ground and twirled her around. The bystanders must have thought that they were a married couple reuniting and not a couple who was technically not in a relationship.

"I know this isn't a fancy place or way of saying it... and I know we still have a lot to learn about each other... but would you officially go on a date with me?" Nathan asked.

"Yes, I will."

"Okay, how about tomorrow?" Nathan eagerly inquired.

"Sounds good. Do you need a ride back home?"

"I've got to take the bus back to do a few last things, and I'll see you tomorrow," Nathan added. "Okay. I'll see you tomorrow. I'm so excited!" Lacy said as she turned around to leave the airport and return home.

However, before she could get much farther than arm's length from Nathan, he took her hand and pulled her back to his chest.

"Wait..."

"Did you forget something?"

"I just want to enjoy this moment a little bit longer," Nathan smirked.

He took her in his arms and kissed her again.

"Hey, Nathan, we know that you could do that all day, but, um, it's time to go," Martin interrupted.

"Okay, be there in a second." Nathan turned back to Lacy. "Bye, Lacy. I'll see you tomorrow."

"Bye." She smiled and blew him a kiss.

Usually, she never liked public displays of affection, PDA, but she made an exception just this one time.

She left with a smile that would stay on her face for days. She wondered if she could already be falling in love with him. She was in dreamland, and so was Nathan. She knew the dreamland would not last, but for the moment, she wanted to stay in the ideal world with nothing else but this new budding romance.

"Well, that was unexpected," Martin commented.

"Yeah, I thought she was in Kansas," Clyde remarked.

Nathan answered in a daze, "Yeah, she was, but she told me that she just moved back."

"Well, I'm glad she caught you before you took a flight to Kansas," JJ said.

"Yeah, me too," Nathan said, still living in la-la land.

"You are totally in love, man."

"Yeah, guys, I think I am." He said as he looked back at her one last time as she slowly drifted from his view.

Chapter Nineteen

They arrived back on base and then crashed once they got home. It felt so good to be in a warm house and a comfy bed once again. The men all fell asleep right away, and the next day, they did not wake up until around noon. When Nathan looked at his phone, he had texts from his parents and from Lacy. He read both texts as his eyes slowly adjusted to staring at the bright light of the screen. As his phone keyboard began to come into focus, Nathan replied to both Lacy and his mother. Lacy asked when they wanted to meet, and he realized he never said when they should meet. He replied, "Just woke up. Maybe we can meet at 2."

"2 it is."

"You're free?" Nathan texted back, surprised that she would be free.

"I just moved here, so I might have some more free time at first."

"Well, lucky me," Nathan added with a wink emoji.

"See you soon."

"See you soon."

Nathan did not need to know it, but Lacy also just woke up from a night of much-needed deep sleep. The last few weeks, she anxiously waited for him to come back from deployment; she had a difficult time sleeping more than five hours each night. Now that she knew he was safe and on home soil, she could have peace again and fall asleep with no problem. She took her time eating breakfast and then looked in her closet for something to wear. She ended up choosing jean shorts and a nice lace tank top, since it was pretty hot in July.

Nathan looked in his dresser and thought of what he should wear. He knew exactly what he would wear every day in the last seven months, and it was always weird to get back to civilian life after deployment. He ended up picking out jean shorts and a plaid button-up shirt. Honestly, he did not even think of where he would take her. He realized he did not quite think it through. The clock turned to 1:30 pm, and he went to pick her up at the address she texted him. It was only about ten minutes from where he lived.

This time he remembered to ring the doorbell and forego the knocking.

"Hi, come in," Lacy said as she finished getting ready.

"Okay."

"So, what are we doing?" Lacy asked curiously.

"To be honest, I didn't think that far."

"That's okay. I did," Lacy said, knowing that he might have replied that way.

"Oh, so what did you have in mind?" Nathan asked curiously.

"I thought that I could show you my favorite place to go."

"Lead the way."

She hopped into the driver's seat, with Nathan in the passenger seat, and headed to the park she used to go to years ago to think. They walked around and talked for hours about everything they missed in each other's lives. It was weird for Lacy to be back in her hometown, and just as she expected, the memories came flooding back. She remembered when she first took James to the park and the multiple times they would come to the park to spend time together. The park was their favorite place to go just about all the time. It was even where James proposed to Lacy. Lacy sharing this special place with Nathan showed that she was starting to move on and be vulnerable with someone again. She could clearly remember the day that James proposed to her.

~ 7 years ago ~

James and Lacy walked around the loop at the park about three times. It started to get dark as they waited for the movies in the park to begin. They would go just about every free weekend, and it was one of their favorite things to do together. The movie started, and it was a brisk evening, so not too many people showed up. Once the movie began, Lacy and James were engrossed in watching it. The park always showed two films, and between the two was time to stretch legs and use the bathroom. James and Lacy got up during the intermission and took another lap around the park. On the way back to the movie spot, James took Lacy down a path to a gazebo. The gazebo in the distance was decorated with different flowers and a string of Christmas lights with a pattern of green and red repeated throughout the whole strand. James took Lacy's hand and led her to the gazebo. She loved the feeling of his hands in hers. It was weird how she went from not liking touch that much to never wanting to let go of James's hand. They walked down the path to the gazebo, and when he got there, he got down on one knee and asked her to marry him. Of course, she said yes. The following week he was deployed, and that was the last time and last memory with him.

~ Present day ~

*L*acy could not help but think about it as she and Nathan went down the path to where the gazebo used to stand. Now, instead of the gazebo, stood a garden area with different varieties of roses.

Nathan noticed that she was deep in thought. "Are you okay?"

"Yeah, sorry, just thinking about some good memories here."

"With James?"

"Yeah, actually, he proposed to me here," she said as they walked around the rose garden.

"Well, then, thank you for sharing this place with me."

"I thought it was about time that I should share it with someone."

"He sounds like he was a very special guy."

"He was... I think if you knew him, y'all would be good friends," Lacy added.

"Yeah, it seems so."

"Speaking of James..." Nathan tiptoed, trying to bring up something that he had been thinking about lately.

"Yes."

"You know that guy I told you about I was trying to save and the thing he said to me before he died." Nathan hesitantly brought it up even though it might ruin the rest of their date.

"Yes, I think so...."

"Well, I had a dream when I was overseas this deployment, and I remembered his name... and it all came back to me so vividly, and the man's name was James... Do you think it was your James?"

"I don't know...." Lacy said with her hands beginning to shake. She did not know what to say. She was in shock. She seemed to be in shock a lot with Nathan around, whether it was something he said or something he did.

"I'm sorry if I just ruined the mood," Nathan said.

"Oh, you didn't... you just got me thinking. Could you describe to me what he looked like?" "He had brown hair, brown eyes; he had a scar on his right hand, and another scar on his left knee and a tattoo with Psalm 23 on his wrist."

"It sounds like him." Lacy did not know what to say. She honestly did not know how she felt at the moment, and, more than anything, she was confused.

"Oh, my gosh... I am so sorry, Lacy."

"Can we go home now? I think this news just took all my energy away."

"Yeah."

They walked back to the car, and not a word was said between the two. All Lacy could think about was *Why did he have to die, and then I end up being with the guy who tried to save him?*

Nathan thought the same thing. *Why couldn't I have saved her fiancé and then we would not be here?... but maybe it had to happen for me to meet my one love.*

He drove back and dropped her off.

"Lacy...again, I'm really sorry." Nathan did not know what else he could say to make this better for her.

"It's not your fault...Just give me some time to grasp this new information."

"Okay. Bye."

As he left, he felt like he just messed up something that could have been great. But at the same time, he did not want to hide this information from her. It would be even more devastating if she found out he held onto the secret. He wanted to be honest, no matter what the outcome would be.

He honestly thought that her reaction would be bigger than it was.

Here I go again, messing everything up, Nathan thought as he drove back to his apartment.

He got back, and no one was home. He crawled into his bed and fell asleep. Three hours later, he heard Clyde opening the door to the apartment. He walked out of his room, and Clyde saw that something was not right.

"Weren't you supposed to have your date with Lacy today?" Clyde said.

"Yeah, I did...."

"And it went that bad?"

"No... it went great...well...until...I brought up about the dream I had when I was overseas about that guy."

"Oh no...And it was her fiancé?"

"Yup."

"Sorry. I thought she would take it well," Clyde said.

"She did the best she could, but she probably just has questions of why."

"So, after that, what happened?"

"I drove her back, and she said she needed time

to process it all. It's just crazy how in a moment every-thing changed."

"Just give her time. I'm sure she will come around."

"Well, I hope so."

"How about we do something to get your mind off it." Clyde was his best friend, and he would always be there to help him through whatever came his way.

"Like what?"

"Nacho and poker night with Martin," Clyde sug-gested.

"What about JJ? Okay, sounds good. Do we have everything?"

"Oh, yeah, we can see. He has been training to get back into shape. I'll ask him. Let me look in the cup-boards and fridge."

Clyde looked and saw that they had everything they needed. "Got it all. I'll just text Martin and JJ and let them know."

"Good."

Later, the guys caught up with JJ on his therapy and how everything was going. JJ shared how, in the beginning, he struggled to want to do anything. Still, he remembered that he needed to persevere if he wanted to get back to his battalion. He knew he had two decisions: give up or move on to get back into shape. After a few days of moping after surgery and recovery time, JJ got up and started to diligently go to therapy. You could see how much he improved within the last few months and his determination to be ready for the next deployment. JJ asked about Lacy, and Nathan gave him a brief version of what transpired since they saw each other.

Then they ate some nachos. These weren't ordinary nachos. They had restaurant-style chips and then topped the nachos with cheese dip, jalapeño peppers, pulled pork, bacon, green peppers, and more. So first, they each got a plate to make the nachos and then started with a poker game. They decided to play a game of Texas hold 'em. Instead of betting money, each poker chip represented a cookie earned. Sometimes they would play with real money, but they would usually end up betting something different each time.

In the first round, JJ got lucky with earning ten poker chips after getting a royal flush. In the next round, Martin got a straight while the other two just only had a high card. They did many rounds of the game, and in the last round, each man went all in. In the end, JJ got lucky and got another royal flush which left him with 30 poker chips to cash in for cookies. He could not eat all those cookies, but it was still fun to play for them. The game made them hungry, so they went for seconds because the nachos were just the right combination of cheesy, salty, sweet goodness.

That was just the beginning of the guys' night.

Chapter Twenty

While the guys were having their night, Lacy went back to her apartment and did nothing. She immediately went to her room and lay on her bed. She felt like she just self-sabotaged her relationship with Nathan. She did not mean to, but the news shocked her so much that she became confused. She did not know what to think or what to do. All she wanted to do at that moment was sleep. In her dreams, she dreamed of James, and at the very end, he said something to her that stuck with her as she woke up. "Lacy, let me go and give him a chance. I don't know why I had to die, but God has a plan."

She woke up startled. It was as if, for a split second, James was right back there with her, and it felt so good. She felt once again conflicted. She thought she had finally made up her mind, but then something new came up, which made her doubt all over again. She put her head back on her pillow and dozed off again. It was not thirty minutes later that she woke up again, and the whole rest of the night, she prayed and battled with what decision to make. In the morning, Lacy rushed over to Nathan's house and hoped to get there before he left for the day. She rang the doorbell and no answer.

"Dude, someone is here," Martin said with a groggy voice.

"Who is here this early in the morning?" Clyde remarked.

"It's not that early; it's 10," Nathan said.

"Too early when you stay up until 3 am," Martin replied.

"Well, should we get the door?" Nathan asked.

"You go get it. We are not presentable," Martin said as Clyde agreed.

"Like I am either." He had shorts on but no shirt.

"More than we are," JJ and Martin exclaimed, since they were just in their boxer shorts. By the time they decided who would get the door, Lacy had already waited for ten minutes. She left a note on the door and turned to leave. Then she got back in her car and drove down the road to her parent's house. Nathan sauntered to the door and opened it. No one was there. He almost walked back in before he saw an envelope on the ground addressed to him. He took a moment to open the letter and read it.

Dear Nathan,

I'm sorry I missed you and I'm sorry about what happened yesterday. I just wanted to stop by and let you know that for real this time my mind is made up. You surprised me yesterday with what you said and I just could not process it. I prayed about it again and more clarity came to me. If you want to talk you know where I'll be.

Love, Lacy

"Guys, we just missed Lacy."

"That's who was at the door?" Clyde said.

"Yeah. I've got to go."

Martin uttered, "Nathan, um..."

But Nathan did not hear a thing because he ran out to his car and went on his way.

Where is she talking about? Nathan thought as he drove down the road. "Oh, I got it! She is at the park!" he said to himself.

He made a left turn and then a right turn. Then he made one last turn into the parking lot. He got out of the car and ran to the rose garden. He wanted to make sure that he got to her before she left. He ran as fast as he could and got there just in time because Lacy was on the move again.

"Lacy!" Nathan yelled.

She did not turn her head.

"Lacy! Wait!" he yelled again.

She turned her head. "You found me!"

"Yes! Stay put!" he continued, out of breath.

"Okay."

She sat down at the bench and waited. A minute later, Nathan walked up and sat next to her. He took her hand and put it in his.

"Lacy, I'm sorry again for what I said yesterday."

"No, Nathan. I'm sorry for how I reacted. Like I said in the note, I was shocked."

"I'm also sorry I didn't get the door on time. We had a late night and just woke up when you rang the bell."

"No worries. I can see that you ran right after me."

"How?"

"You are still in your pajamas, and you forgot to put a shirt on. You are looking really rugged and handsome."

"Wait, what... that must have been what Martin and Clyde tried to tell me."

"I mean, not many people are here. This might be your best look yet," Lacy chuckled.

"Very funny. So can we try this again?"

"Yes, and I will do my best not to change my mind again."

"Will you be my girlfriend? I know that it is sudden and only after one date, but I just think that it is right."

"Yes."

They sealed the moment with a kiss, and that was when the real adventure began.

Chapter Twenty-One-The Wedding

Another month went by, and it was already the beginning of August. During the final wedding planning for Cody and Hannah, Catherine and Quinn had a baby girl at the end of July whom they named Crystal. Crystal was born at 7 lbs 5 oz, and from the very moment Lacy saw her niece, she fell in love with her. She had dark brown hair and bright blue eyes. Even though she was a baby, you could see joy in her eyes. Catherine went into labor just two weeks before the wedding, so Catherine could not make it to the wedding since she was still recovering and taking care of the baby.

Meanwhile, in that same month, Lacy continued planning Cody and Hannah's wedding. She knew from the very beginning that Hannah always wanted a wedding based on the movie *Tangled*. She took that into account with the decorations for both the wedding and the reception. They both worked hard to get everything ready. A week before the wedding, the family came together to transform the wedding venue into her *Tangled* wonderland.

On the day of the wedding, the weather was nothing but blue skies. It was not too hot and not too cold. The wedding took place outside in the afternoon in the heat of the day. The aisle outside was lined with lit lanterns as Hannah would walk down the aisle. At the front of the aisle was a flower arch decked out with purple, white, pink, and yellow flowers. The white chairs were lined in perfect formation with flowers loosely draped over the back of each one. As the guests came in, they saw a sign with the words "Best Day Ever" and the wedding date 08/10. Before the bridal party walked down the aisle, a white aisle runner was put down for them to walk on. The aisle runner was covered in lace and as thin as a piece of paper, so it was the perfect material for Hannah to walk on to not mess up her wedding dress or shoes. The bridesmaids walked down the aisle in their light-colored chiffon, spaghetti-strapped, purple dresses that fell to the ankles. As Lacy walked down the aisle, she locked eyes on Nathan, who was in the middle row closest to the aisle on the bride's side. Lacy could not help but wonder if this would be her in a year or so. Then the ring bearer, Cody's nephew, three years old, turning four in a few months, walked down in his white shirt, little suspenders, and light blue pants. After walking halfway down the aisle, his nephew started running to the front with excitement on his face. It was a sight to see. Everyone in the audience began to laugh as he made it to the front of the aisle.

Next, the two flower girls, Cody's nieces, walked down the aisle with small baskets covered in purple petals on the outside and filled up with light purple petals. The flower girls looked so cute in their purple tutu dresses, and they put on a show as they walked down the aisle, twirling around as if they were ballerinas. Then everyone stood up as Hannah walked down the aisle. Her dress looked like something out of a princess movie; she beamed as she walked down the aisle in a strapless ballgown style that flowed below her ankles. A close examination would reveal the perfect beading on the bodice.

In the front, Cody's eyes filled with tears as he watched his bride walk down the aisle. He was dressed in a white shirt with purple suspenders to match the wedding color. He had never seen anything so beautiful and could not believe that she was about to be his wife.

Hannah walked down the aisle with such grace despite her long train. Her hair was in a braid with flowers placed to make it look just like Rapunzel in the movie. She literally looked like a spitting image of her.

Once everyone sat down, the ceremony began, and the couple exchanged their vows. They had decided to recite the traditional vows and then say some of their own words, too. At the end, the minister prayed over the marriage. Hannah was in awe of how the wedding went, and she could not imagine how long Lacy took to make everything perfect for her.

It started to get darker outside, and everyone walked down the path to the reception held inside. In the reception ballroom, each table had a white linen tablecloth.

In the center was a lit lantern with the table number on it. Also, from the ceiling hung small glass holders with lighted LED candles so that they looked like little lanterns in the sky. The lights were dimmed inside so that everyone could feel as if they were at the lantern festival in the movies. There was a little chalkboard at the bar area that stated they were at "The Snuggly Duckling, where even Ruffians & Thugs have dreams," just like the tavern in the movie.

A bit later, the guests were asked to sit down as the bride and groom were introduced. This was when Lacy finally got a chance to slip away to talk to Nathan.

"Hey, sorry, this is the first time we could talk," Lacy said as she came over to Nathan.

"I understand. Might I say that the purple in that dress makes you look spectacular?"

"Thank you."

"Oh my gosh... you actually took that compliment better."

"I'm trying."

"Has it hit you yet... that your sister is married?"

"Not yet... it's crazy."

The host interrupted them by explaining that dinner was about to be served and everyone needed to find their seat. Cody and Hannah decided to just have a sweetheart table, so Lacy walked with Nathan to their table. The dinner choice was chicken with steamed broccoli and roasted potatoes served on a frying pan in honor of the movie. It was a simple meal; however, it tasted delicious. Then the best man, Luke, gave his speech.

"Well, hello everyone. What can I say about the groom? Oh, boy, I could say a lot, but we don't have enough time for that. Anyways, man, Cody, you've been my friend since the day we could walk. You've been with me through the horrible years, the years of confusion, and all the other years in-between. Thank you for being a great friend. As for Hannah, you changed Cody to be an even better man than he already was. And I mean, I was there from the very beginning of your relationship as the guy sitting next to Cody in class. I mean, folks, I saw it all. Anyways, I wish you all the best luck in your marriage."

Then the maid of honor, Lacy, gave an amazing, sincere speech to her sister and her new husband. "Hannah, there is so much to say. I can't believe that my younger sister is getting married so soon. Cody, you have an amazing woman here who loves you and, even more importantly, loves the Lord. I've practically followed your relationship since the beginning, and, Cody, I'm excited to have another brother in the family. Your love is just starting, and I can't wait to see what lies ahead. Hannah, you have been my best friend since practically the day you were born, and as we've gotten older, I've enjoyed how much closer we are. You have been my confidant through thick and thin. Love both of you and wish you the best in your marriage."

Then, like any traditional wedding, it was time for the father-daughter and mother-son dances. After that, the dance floor became livelier, with more family members joining and the children twirling and dancing. There was a photo booth in another part of the room with a wanted sign cut out, and at the bottom, instead of the frame, it said what the reward was: "Being too awesome." Nathan and Lacy snuck to this room to take some goofy pictures before returning to their table to finish dinner. Nathan took one last bite of his food and then asked Lacy to dance.

Lacy replied, "Okay…but I'm warning you that I'm not the best dancer."

"I doubt that."

He took her hand, and they walked hand-in-hand to the dance floor. He led the dance with one hand on her back and the other on her shoulder. They danced and danced until it was time for the cake to be cut.

Hannah and Cody gathered around the cake and worked together to cut the first piece. The cake was a traditional cake on the outside and untraditional on the inside. On the outside, the cake was covered with white icing, and then the symbol of the sun was intricately detailed. In addition, each guest also got a pascal cake pop with their piece of cake. The first tier was lemon raspberry filling, while the second tier of the cake was filled with chocolate gauche. Cody and Hannah each took a piece of the cake. There was a moment of hesitation before Hannah smashed her piece of the cake all over Cody's face. He had it just about everywhere but his eyes and ears. Then it was Cody's turn, and he was not any nicer. Cody took the piece of cake and smashed it all over her face, and even got it in a strand of her hair. Hannah and Cody kissed and then went to the bathroom to clean up.

When they got back, more dancing happened for a few more hours. Some dancers just rocked back and forth and others got on the dance floor to breakdance. One of the groomsmen showed off with breakdancing, and then the little boys tried to copy him. The little boys were so cute trying to mimic the others with their dance moves, and for their first time, they did a pretty good job.

After hours of dancing, it was time to send off the couple. The sendoff was definitely Lacy's favorite part of the wedding, especially since it surprised everyone except her. She asked all the guests to come outside and then gave each a sky lantern. As the couple walked out for the sendoff, the guests lifted up their lanterns and sent them off into the night sky. Then before they left, Hannah and Cody took the last lantern and sent it off into the night sky. The sky lit up with all the floating lanterns and ended a perfect day. Hannah and Cody walked hand-in-hand into their getaway car and headed off to a new life together.

Chapter Twenty-Two

The next three months flew by...

Lacy met with a couple who needed a wedding planner, and that wedding led to a dozen more after that. After that wedding, her business in Virginia grew even faster than she ever thought possible. Soon, she was busy planning multiple weddings and needed to hire some employees to help. Also, in Kansas, Rose and Susan earned their respect as event planners, and the business continued to thrive over there as well, more than she thought possible in just a short amount of time. It was so exciting how much things changed and grew so fast.

Nathan trained most of the day. He got to visit his parents for a week, and that was the first time since he was deployed that Lacy and Nathan were apart. Ever since he asked her to be his girlfriend, they basically saw each other at least three times a week. On the second date, Nathan took Lacy to his favorite place, near Washington DC. Amid the hustle and bustle of the city, Nathan had found this running path that he loved to go to when he got the chance. He shared the place with Lacy, and she loved it. He thought that maybe that could be their place since the other park was hers and

James'. As Nathan and Lacy walked down the trail, they found a hidden trail. They followed it until they arrived at a meadow filled with beautiful flowers of all sizes and colors. It was like they were walking into a natural botanical garden in the middle of the city. Instantly, Lacy fell in love with the place almost as easily as it was to fall in love with Nathan. Each time they were together, something just felt right. It was more than that actually; she had this peace once again that Nathan was the right one for her. Lacy could be vulnerable with him more than anyone else she knew, and she felt after four months that she was in love with him. She just had to find the right words to say.

In addition, Nathan's parents moved to Virginia to be closer to their son. They battled with the decision while he was deployed and then finally made their final decision in September. They had just retired, so more opportunities became open to them, and they decided to go for it. They missed a lot of Nathan's life the last ten years, so moving close to him was a way to make up for it. In November, a week before Thanksgiving, his parents moved into their new house. The house was not as big as Lacy's parents' house, but it would suffice for the two of them. They rented a one-story house with just the right amount of space and an amazing backyard for their new dog to run around in. His parents decided the day they retired to get a dog from the shelter. They went and picked out this adorable five-year-old yellow Labrador retriever, and they fell in love with him instantly. He was named Max at the shelter, but they changed the name to Leo. It fit him. They stayed busy training him, and by Thanksgiving, Leo could listen to any command. It was perfect because he would get his first test run at Winter's Thanksgiving dinner.

Chapter Twenty-Three
2ⁿᵈ Thanksgiving

It was Thanksgiving Day once again. Nathan rang the doorbell at Lacy's apartment to pick her up for the day.

"Hello, beautiful!"

Lacy was dressed in a navy-blue jumpsuit this time. She had her hair up in a nice bun. She and Nathan were color-coordinated this time, so he wore a white dress shirt with a navy-blue tie. Nathan got a haircut, and the beard that formed over the last few months was now the perfect amount of scruff. Lacy liked a little scruff, but only certain men could pull off a full-on beard.

"Nathan, can you believe it has already been a year since we first met," Lacy reminded him.

"No, it feels like I've known you longer."

"Same."

"If you asked me last year before we met if we would ever be here, I would've thought it was crazy."

"Yes, I would have said the same thing."

"So, are you ready to meet my parents?"

"I'm nervous. From what you told me, they sound

lovely, and I'm sure everything will be fine."

"You don't need to worry. They know so much about you already, and they already love you."

"Thanks for the encouragement."

They arrived at her parent's house. A few minutes later, another knock interrupted the conversations inside.

"Lacy, I'm so sorry I didn't warn them." Nathan could see that she was having PTSD again as before. He took her hand and brought her in for an embrace. "Are you okay?"

"I'm going to be. I'm sorry; just give me a minute."

"I'm such an idiot. I should've told them."

"It's okay; they couldn't know. I'll be right back."

Lacy went upstairs to go take a few deep breaths and compose herself. Nathan took hold of the knob on the door and opened it to see his parents. They embraced for a while, and then Nathan invited them in.

"Mom and Dad, the rest of the family is coming over soon, and Lacy will be down in a second. If you want to come in the kitchen, I can introduce you to Lacy's mom and dad."

They followed him into the kitchen, and he introduced them to Lacy's parents.

"Mom and Dad, this is Lacy's parents."

"It is nice to meet you," they said to each other as they shook hands.

"I've heard so much about you from Nathan. It is

great to finally meet you," said Lacy's mom.

"Do you need any help?" Nathan's mom asked.

"Oh, no. We have just about everything done here. You are our guests and make yourself at home."

"I heard that your family plays an annual football game. That sounds fun." Nathan's dad remarked.

"Oh, it is! Lacy is actually one of our best players. Speaking of Lacy, where is she?" Lacy's dad said.

"Will you excuse me for a second? I'm going to go upstairs and make sure everything is okay,"

Lacy's mom said.

"Of course," said Lucy, Nathan's mom.

Once her mom left, Nathan's parents headed into the family room to talk to Nathan while waiting for Lacy.

"Hey, son, maybe you should check on Lacy. Is there a reason she wouldn't be okay?" Lucy said.

"It's not my place to say."

"Oh," they said with curious looks on their faces.

Lacy's mom found Lacy upstairs in her room, crying her eyes out.

"Mom, I thought that I got past this. It's been six years now, and honestly, I love Nathan." "Honey, just because you still are dealing with flashbacks doesn't make you love Nathan any less. Eventually, someday you might be healed of your flashbacks, but it takes time."

"I know. It's just I didn't expect to start off this day by crying my eyes out right before his parents came. As much as I have tried to stop, they just keep on coming."

"Take a few deep breaths. I will go downstairs and explain that you will be down soon."

"Thanks, mom."

Her mom came back downstairs and smiled at Nathan's parents in the family room. "Lacy will be down in a few minutes. Thanks for your patience. It's not my place either to tell you what is going on, but she will explain it if she feels up to it."

"Okay..." his parents said now with a puzzled look.

Then Lacy's mom walked back into the kitchen and whispered to her husband about Lacy. About ten minutes later, Lacy came downstairs looking the best she could with the current circumstances. Nathan introduced her to his mom and dad. Lacy shook his mom's hand and then his dad's. Then she began to apologize.

"Mr. and Mrs. Thompson, I'm so sorry that you had to wait. You are probably wondering what is going on and I'd like to tell you. I'm sorry this is your first impression of me."

"Honey, no worries. Actually, to be honest, I already think you are a great woman based off of what Nathan has said to me," Nathan's mom stated.

"Well, um, long story short is that my fiancé died six years ago yesterday, and I have PTSD with certain things like whenever I hear a knock on the door, and it floods all back."

"Oh, we are very sorry. We didn't mean to...."

"Oh, no, it's not your fault; you know, actually your son did it last year... It's what started our conversation. Anyways, it is nice to meet you, and I've heard so much about you from Nathan; I feel like I practically already know you."

"I heard that you've been quite busy with your sister's wedding and then your business taking off here."

"Yes. I thought it would take longer for it to grow since I had so many clients in Kansas, but I'm amazed how easily it picked up here."

"I saw pictures of some of your weddings, and they are absolutely gorgeous. Can I ask if you will do your own wedding design?"

"Can I be honest? I haven't really thought about it. I would probably say yes... but I'm not sure." By this time, Nathan and his dad were having another conversation about Nathan's last deployment and what he has been doing since. They could not hear a word, and so the conversation continued.

"So, I know this might be too soon, but can you see yourself marrying my son? We heard about last Thanksgiving when Nathan came, and he told us so much. I could hear it in his voice that he might be in love, so I thought I'd ask."

"Yes, I know that I could."

"Good, because I've never seen him happier."

"I haven't told him yet, but I love him, and I never imagined it could happen again."

"I'm glad that you could, and again I am terribly sorry for the loss of your fiancé."

"Thank you. I was really nervous to meet you, but you've made me feel at ease."

In just a few minutes, dinner was ready. Catherine and Quinn and little baby Crystal showed up just in time. It would just be them this Thanksgiving, as Hannah and Cody decided to spend Thanksgiving with Cody's parents. Little baby Crystal looked so cute in her fall onesie.

They all walked to the table. Catherine put Crystal in her little carrier so that she could be near the table. Lacy's dad carried the turkey on the platter into the dining room and placed it at the center of the table. Then Lacy and Nathan brought the rest of the side dishes in with the help of Quinn.

The meal was delicious. The company was even better. This year, no awkward questions got asked, and Quinn did not make Nathan feel uncomfortable. The conversation flowed with details about the last few months of activities happening in the families' lives.

"Wow, you had a lot going on," Nathan's mom said.

"Yeah, we have been very busy. It's been one thing after the other," Lacy's mom replied.

"And now it looks like we have something else to look forward to...maybe next year," Nathan's mom said with a smirk across her face.

"Oh, yes, maybe...." Lacy's mom said with a smile

written across her face.

Lacy overheard. "Hey, both of you, stop meddling," she remarked with a joking tone.

"Okay...okay."

Soon dinner was over, and it was time for the football game. The family had two fewer key players, but they would have to do with what they had. Nathan's parents were advised ahead of time if they wanted to be part of the game to bring a change of clothes. Everyone went to different parts of the house and changed. Lacy's mom and Catherine did not play because they both watched the 4-month old baby. There would be a lot fewer players this year: Quinn, Lacy, Lacy's dad, Nathan, and a new recruit, Nathan's dad. Nathan's mom decided that she would just watch the game because she was not very good at football and did not want to try to keep up with the young ones.

They decided again to just play two-hand touch, and the game felt weird with the lack of players. The first team was Quinn and Lacy. The other team was Nathan and Lacy's dad, and Nathan's dad would alternate. It was two-on-two, which made it pretty obvious who the ball would be thrown or given to. They still had a good game and a lot of funny moments. One of the best moments was when Lacy caught a pass on the one-yard line that Quinn threw from the 20-yard line and then ran in for a touchdown. Even with a smaller group, both teams stayed super competitive, and in the end, they almost tied. However, Nathan got the ball from his dad, and he ran in for a touchdown without anyone stopping him. Lacy tried to reach him, but he ran too fast. When she got there, it was too late.

This time, Nathan did not have to rush off and stayed for dessert. He got to try one of Lacy's famous apple pies, which changed his life forever.

"Wow, Lacy, this is amazing. This is the real reason I'm dating you...."

"Oh, finally the truth comes out," she bantered back.

"You two are adorable," Catherine commented.

"Yeah, they are definitely made for each other," Nathan's mom said with Lacy's mom in agreement.

The day turned into night, and it was time for the group to leave. Nathan and Lacy, along with her parents, were the only ones who stayed for their annual Christmas movie night. It seemed that things were changing and that each year it was going to be different. They would try to hold on to the traditions, but circumstances did not make it feel the same anymore. Before the movie started, Lacy asked if she could talk to Nathan outside. They walked to the backyard and sat down on the patio.

"What's up?" Nathan asked.

"Nathan, I got to tell you something really important!"

"Wait, I want to go first!"

"Okay… if you insist."

"Lacy, I think I know what you are going to say… at least I hope I know what you are going to say, and I want to go first."

"Okay, go for it!"

"I love you. I've loved you since that first day when I saw you standing in front of me. Throughout that day, as we talked and I got to know you more, I knew that you were someone special. As I've got to know you the last year, my love for you has truly grown more than I ever expected. I think I finally know what love is and what it is like to be in love."

"I love you, too! I can't believe that I'm even saying that. I can't believe that I'm here at this moment. I would've never expected anything like this. I know I've said it before, but it is true. I thought my one and only love would be James, but God was able to heal my heart."

"I'm glad he did."

He took her in his arms, told him he loved her again, and then they kissed passionately. Neither of them wanted this moment to end.

"It is time for the movie," they heard Lacy's mom say from inside.

"We should probably go in before they catch us out here," Lacy noted.

"Yeah, that would be awkward," Nathan agreed.

Lacy and Nathan walked back into the room and

sat on the couch together. They cuddled up near each other and got ready to watch the Christmas movie.

Chapter Twenty-Four

The following year leading up to the next Thanksgiving would fly by even quicker than the one before. Lacy flew back and forth to Kansas only a few times a year. Her business in Virginia continued to grow tremendously. Once again, she was busier than ever and had to hire two more employees to make it four total to work on multiple events at a time. Nathan continued to train to be ready in case he got deployed again. He would be at the base just about every day. It started to be more difficult for them to find time to be with each other. They took any chance that they could take to slip away from their jobs and spend some much-needed time together. Things got even more serious by Christmas, and Lacy wondered if he would propose even after five months of dating. The proposal did not come, and after reflecting, she was okay with it.

At the beginning of April, Nathan went to work thinking he would propose to Lacy the next month. However, he did not know that the same day, he would get the news that he would be deployed again. He would miss their one year together. Also, he was concerned that he would not be back for the following Thanksgiving due to his deployment. It was as if, in an instant, everything had changed. He thought long and hard about if he should propose before he left or if he should wait until after. In the end, his mind was made up that he would wait. He thought about how James had asked her a few months before he was deployed, and he did not want Lacy to feel like the same thing would happen all over again. When he got the news, the first person he wanted to tell was Lacy, and when he got the chance, that was exactly what he did. They both had the evening off a week before he would leave, and he wanted to make it extra special because it was probably the last time they would spend time together before he was deployed. He called her right after he heard the news.

"Hey, Lacy! Can we have dinner tomorrow?"

"Yes, I would love that!"

"Great. I'll pick you up after work."

"Okay. Love you."

The next day came quicker than expected. Nathan picked her up after work, and they went to a new taco restaurant that had just opened down the street from his house.

"Hey, how was your day?" Nathan asked.

"It was busy but good. I got to finish getting ready for the anniversary party tomorrow, and I also started sketching out some ideas with my team for a wedding that will be the day before Christmas of this year. How was yours?"

"It was good, but I have some news...."

"I already assumed so."

"Well... if what you assumed is that I'm being deployed, then you are correct."

"When do you leave?"

"Two weeks."

"And I'm going to Kansas next week, so you are thinking this probably is the last time we will see each other before you leave."

"Yes, and I wanted to have the time to be with you and pray with you and just make sure you are going to be okay."

"You know... that every time you will leave, it will be a challenge, but I am trusting God that I can find peace."

"This might be the same as before where I have some communication, but not all the time."

"I think that I might have more peace this time than before. God is working on me even more since Thanksgiving."

"That is good to hear. I can't imagine what is going through your head, and I just thought that we could take this time to pray for this next chapter in our lives."

So first, they had a meal, and then they went to the church to pray. It was such a nice day outside that they ended up walking to the prayer garden just on the side of the church. It was similar to Lacy's special place at the park but a little bit smaller.

Nathan and Lacy held each other's hands and began to pray.

Nathan started: *Dear Lord, thank you for how you've brought both of us together and how you are healing and have healed both of us. I ask that as I go overseas, you watch over my whole battalion and that you give each and every one of us guidance. Lord, I ask that Lacy can be filled with your peace while I am on deployment. I ask that she knows and remembers who you are and that you are always there no matter what happens in my life or hers. You are in control, and you are there for us in all circumstances. Lord, I pray that this time apart from each other grows us, most importantly closer to you, but also that we grow closer to each other. That this distance doesn't make us distant, but that it renews and makes our relationship even stronger.*

He finished, and Lacy closed her eyes and began her prayer.

"Lord, I ask for the safety of the ones I love. I pray that I can have peace that you will take care of Nathan and keep everyone in his battalion safe. I pray that I don't look to the worst-case scenario but that I thrive only on the truth in front of me. I don't think about the past and worry that it will happen again, but that I cast all my worries onto you. Lord, I ask that in the hardest moments is when I feel you reassuring me and comforting me the most. I pray for his whole battalion and all those that are overseas keeping our country

safe. Lord, I pray that they can find the light even in the midst of all the darkness of war, that they know that you are the best prize and best person to have on their side. Lord, please watch over all those who have lost their lives and the spouses and family members who have to live with that forever. I pray over my relationship with Nathan, that I trust in you and that we put you first always in our relationship."

They sat there with Lacy's head on Nathan's shoulder and continued to just pray to the Lord. A few hours later, when the sun began to set, they got up and headed back to Nathan's car.

He parked his car in front of her apartment building and walked her to her room.

"Well, this is it. I love you, and I'm going to miss you so much," Nathan said.

"Ditto."

"Really, that is all you are going to say at this moment?"

"No... I love you, and I'm going to miss you more than you could ever know."

They hugged for probably the next five minutes, holding on to each other and making up for all the time they would be apart. Then Nathan leaned in for a kiss.

"I don't want to leave," Nathan said as he leaned close to her.

"Me either... but we need to."

"I know."

"Bye."

"Bye."

Before Nathan left, he leaned back in and kissed her one more time.

"I'll see you in seven months."

"I'll be waiting."

And just like that, he was off. Lacy watched him as he walked down the hallway and out the door.

"Lord, I'm trusting you to keep him safe."

She heard a faint voice say back to her, *He is going to be safe. Trust in me.*

At that moment, she knew it was God telling her everything would be just fine.

Chapter Twenty-Five

During his deployment, Nathan and Lacy wrote letters as much as they could, and not once did a letter get lost. Also, this time around, they were able to video chat a few times. It was never a long time, but it was still nice to see each other face to face. Nathan shared on one of their video chats about a woman whom he treated. She stepped on an IED, and it was touch and go for a while, but in the end, she was able to keep one of her legs while the other one got amputated. She could hear in his voice how each death that happened hit him because he blamed himself for the lives lost. She wished she could do something more than tell him everything will be okay, but it was hard when they were that far apart.

Lacy shared about weddings she worked on and how everything went. She thought at least telling him the good things happening in her life would help him for the time being to think good thoughts and not focus on all the lives lost. The last time they got to talk, she reassured him that he was making a difference and that it was not his fault. They spent time praying with each other again before saying goodbye. That was the last time that she would hear from him for a while.

Sometimes she wondered how anyone could go through traumatic experiences like that and still live a normal life. She saw not only in him but in all the military that they had the resiliency to keep going, no matter the battle they faced inside. The rest of his deployment left little time for him to write or video chat with her. He tried, but they were busy fighting overseas to take the time to write a letter back. He got some of her letters, and it was the only thing that kept him going the remainder of his deployment.

Chapter Twenty-Six
The Following Thanksgiving

It was the day before Thanksgiving, and Nathan was supposed to get back a week before, but there was no news about his battalion arriving anytime soon. She heard the voice of God saying that everything would be okay, and during most of his deployment, she had peace until now. It was the day before Thanksgiving, which also meant that it had now been seven years since James died on this very day. She was feeling every kind of emotion: happy, joyful, worried, scared, and more. She wanted to believe everything was okay, but everything else in her was worried that history was about to repeat itself. She heard a knock at her door and, for the first time since Lacy could remember, for some reason, she did not get a flashback about seven years ago. She opened the door to see none other than her man Nathan standing at the door with a smile written across her face. For a moment, she thought it was a dream. Then Nathan took her in his arms, and she knew that she was not dreaming. She pulled away, confused that he did not contact her earlier.

"When did you get in?"

"I got in yesterday late."

"Why were y'all delayed?"

"Some bad weather. I'm so sorry...Oh, and I just realized I knocked. I cannot believe... I guess I was just so excited."

"Don't worry about it. I was thinking the worst... but nothing matters now that you are here."

"I wanted to tell you so bad, but there was no way of getting in contact with you."

Lacy stopped talking and went in for a kiss.

"Wow, you are being bold," Nathan said.

"I learned from the best."

"Also, I'm done with being a medic. I officially retired from the Navy."

"Wow. This is a shock.

"It was time. I'm ready for the next part of my life in work and in love. I experienced a lot over there, and I don't think I can go back."

"You sure?"

"I'm more sure than anything."

"Okay! I'm excited!"

They moved to the couch and cuddled for hours, enjoying the warm embrace. The only time they did not hold each other was if one of them had to use the bathroom or get up to stretch and move around. He spent the night in the guest room.

In the morning, they headed to her parent's house again for Thanksgiving. Nathan's parents came again, and this time, Nathan's aunt came as well. The Winters' house was decked inside and out with Christmas decorations and lights. This time, the whole family was there since Cody and Hannah alternated between each family's house every other year.

At the dinner table, Nathan's dad said grace, and then everyone dished up some turkey and sides onto their plates. It was the usual side dishes, except this time, Nathan's parents brought a different kind of stuffing, sweet potato casserole, and some breadcrumb mac & cheese. The mac & cheese soon disappeared before making it a second time around the table. It was definitely a great new addition to the meal. The conversation continued all around the table, and they each took turns talking about what they were thankful for. Lacy looked around the table and loved seeing the new additions to the family. She could not wait to see how her family would continue to grow over the next several years. She could not ask for anything better than the family sitting around the table engrossed in conversation. They finished dinner and, before playing the game this year, they took extra time to digest their food by playing a game of Spicy Uno.

Then everyone got changed for the game. Lacy wore a tank top with "#1" printed on the front of the tank top and then gray athletic shorts that went halfway down her thigh. The football game began, and it was once again a close game. However, about halfway through the game, something unexpected happened. Lacy caught the football in the end zone. She proceeded to do a touchdown dance when Nathan came up behind her. She turned around to see Nathan down on one knee with a ring in his hand. She knew it would be coming soon and probably this day, but she had no clue exactly when. She stared at him as he asked her the most important question he could ever ask her at the time.

"It would make me the happiest person in the world. Will you marry me and be my wife?"

Without any hesitation, Lacy said, "Yes!"

The rest of the family gathered around the newly engaged couple and time stood still for a moment. It was a journey to get there... but she finally arrived at her happily-ever-after, despite all the obstacles along the way.

Epilogue

*E*ight months later. It was the day of Nathan and Lacy's wedding. The last few nights, she worked with her family and co-workers to make the reception venue a magical place. Yes, even though it was her wedding, Lacy wanted to be in charge of the decorations. Lacy double-checked the decorations at the reception and then drove over to the wedding venue. As she walked to the field, she took in the beauty of everything. The wedding venue was located in a botanical garden. The natural beauty of the botanical gardens left little need for any other decorations other than white chairs in four rows on each side of the aisle. Lacy decided that she would forego the aisle runner and just walk in the grass. To go with the theme, some flower petals were already scattered down the aisle. Since no one was there, she took a little practice walk down the aisle because she was so fearful of tripping on her way down the aisle.

"Lacy! You need to start getting ready!" Hannah yelled from a distance.

Lacy jumped. She did not think anyone was there. "Hannah. You scared me."

"Sorry, but your wedding is in two hours, and you

need to get your hair done."

"Coming."

Lacy took one last look and turned around. She walked back to the house near the botanical gardens and to the room where she would get ready. She sat down for her sister-in-law, Catherine, to do her hair. Catherine first curled her hair and then pinned it up into a nice updo so that all her hair would be up and out of the way. The bridesmaids worked on getting ready during this time and putting on their navy-blue chiffon dresses. Then after an hour, all that was left was to put her wedding dress on.

At the same time, the groomsmen arrived already dressed in their white dress shirts with gray suspenders and gray dress pants. They found Nathan in a different room of the house, putting on his navy-blue uniform just picked up from the dry cleaner earlier that morning. He looked in the mirror, reflecting on all Lacy and he had been through together in the last couple of years. His groomsmen took that time to ask him if they could pray for him. They laid their hands on his pristine uniform, trying not to leave any wrinkles. Clyde began to open in a word of prayer.

"Dear Lord, Father, I pray for Nathan and Lacy and their journey of marriage. I pray that they live for you and serve you. I pray that you will be with them every step of the way, and they will

come to you with every little thing. Lord, I pray for a marriage with love that continues to grow and understanding and patience with one another. I thank you for bringing us to this moment today, and I pray for provision in this marriage. We never thought we would make it here, and so, Lord, thank you for your protection to make it to this day to see this love that is found in you.

"Amen."

Nathan and the boys finished praying. Each groomsman gave him one last hug before they left the room and made their way to the front of the aisle. By this time, the guests started to arrive and found a place to sit on either side of the aisle. Lacy and Nathan both agreed that there did not have to be a bride and groom side.

Back in the house, Lacy grabbed her off-the-shoulder chiffon wedding dress from the hanger and stepped into it. Her dress was simple but elegant, falling just to her ankles. She had Hannah help zip up the back of her dress, and then she looked in the mirror one last time. They all were ready for the wedding.

"Lacy, ready to go?" her dad said after knocking on the door.

"Yes, Dad, we are ready."

"Okay, I was told to tell everyone that it is time."

Before they left, the bridesmaids surrounded Lacy

and laid their hands on her. They surrounded her just for a minute to pray for the marriage and for God to use their marriage for His glory. The bridesmaids went first, and then Lacy stopped before she would be seen by any of the guests or the groom.

At the front of the aisle, Nathan stood shaking. He had his best man Clyde standing by his side along with his other groomsmen, JJ and Martin. The bridesmaids, Hannah, the matron of honor, Catherine, and another close friend from college started to walk down the aisle one at a time. They carried small bouquets of daisies that were actually picked from Lacy's garden back at her apartment. Lacy wanted it to be really simple. Then Catherine's little girl Crystal, now 2 years old, walked down the aisle in her adorable flower girl dress. She held her small basket and started to scatter the blue and white petals across the grass aisle as she walked down. Next, the ring bearer, the son of one of Lacy's cousins, walked down in a small dress shirt, gray pants, and gray suspenders. He was like a mini-groomsmen.

The wedding song came on, and everyone stood up to see the bride proceed down the aisle. Lacy took one last glance at the beautiful variety of flowers surrounding her and continued to walk towards the aisle. When she got to the start of the aisle, she locked eyes with Nathan in his navy-blue pressed uniform and started to tear up. It was a bittersweet moment. She was ready to marry Nathan, but she could not help, for just a second, to think of James and what could have been. Her dad hooked his arm on hers and walked her down the aisle. She let the thoughts subside, proceeded down the aisle, her eyes hooked on Nathan's. She felt like the luckiest girl in the world. He was struck by her beauty. He thought she looked beautiful in sweatpants and rarely saw her all dressed up. He thought she looked stunning, and he could not take his eyes off of her. It reminded him of the first time he saw her over 2 ½ years ago. He knew then, and he knew now that his life was forever changed.

When she got to the front, the pastor asked, "Who gives this woman away to be married to this man?"

Her mom answered, "We do."

Her dad kissed her on the cheek and said, "Love you."

Lacy took Nathan's hand as her own hand shook in his. Nathan felt his heart beating so fast. He was so in love with her. They turned towards each other, and he easily got lost in her eyes. Lacy handed her daisy bouquet over to Hannah. The pastor started with a prayer as everyone bowed their heads. Then the ceremony began. Nathan and Lacy felt like they were the only ones there. Both could not stop smiling.

The pastor read some Bible verses about everlasting love and then announced, "Okay, everyone. Nathan and Lacy have decided to recite their own vows."

Nathan went first. "Lacy. Where do I start? I never

thought that an invite to a Thanksgiving dinner would change my life. I knew from the moment I saw you that there was something beautiful and broken about you. I just hoped that I would be able to heal that beautiful broken heart. I was lucky enough to fall in love with you but more lucky that you would give me a chance. We have something that I never thought I would ever find. You are my best friend, and I can't wait to be your confidant, for as long as we live, through the laughter, which there will be lots of, and through the tears. I love you more than you could ever know." As he finished, he placed the ring on her finger.

He wanted to lean in and kiss her right then, but he resisted. She was so beautiful. It did not help that she was smiling and had not stopped since she walked down the aisle.

Lacy followed with her vows. "Nathan, I couldn't imagine three years ago that I would ever be in this place with you right now. You made me feel love I never thought I could feel again. You are so patient. I love you so much, and you are my best friend. The Lord gave me a second chance at love, and I couldn't imagine my life without you. Who knew that a Thanksgiving visit would change my whole world? I can't wait to grow old with you and fall in love with you each day over and over again." Then she placed the ring on Nathan's left finger.

The pastor then said, "I now pronounce you husband and wife. You may kiss the bride."

Nathan no longer hesitated. He went in and kissed her like the first time they saw each other after his deployment. Then the ceremony finished with Nathan's dad praying for their marriage and life together.

Hannah handed the bridal bouquet back to Lacy before the recessional. The recessional started with Nathan and Lacy dancing up down the aisle to their favorite upbeat country song. The bridesmaids and groomsmen followed one at a time. They all met back at the house, and it was time for pictures. The botanical gardens were the perfect background for wedding pictures. They got all the photoshoots with the wedding party before the wedding party left to go to the reception.

Lacy and Nathan had some serious photos taken and then started goofing off with each other. Nathan picked Lacy up unexpectedly off the ground where her head was above his and twirled around with her. It was a great moment, and the photographer got a perfect shot. The photographer took another photo of them skipping together with flowers on both sides of them. There was one photo left to take. Nathan took the football on the ground for the photoshoot and threw it to Lacy. She caught the ball. The photographer got every part of the sequence of events. In the photograph, Nathan ran to Lacy to grab her in his arms and carry her to the car that would take them to the reception.

At the reception, people had the time of their lives dancing and enjoying the potluck meal. The rest of the night was a blast, and they enjoyed every minute of it. Lacy threw her bridal bouquet, and little Crystal caught it. Everyone laughed and knew for a fact that Crystal would not be the next one to get married. They left the reception area with a tunnel of sparklers to take them to their getaway car. The night ended with Nathan and Lacy driving away to the next chapter of their lives together. A chapter full of new memories, both good and bad, full of laughter and tears, and lots of fun and exciting new experiences together.

Acknowledgments

I could have never gotten to this point without multiple people in my life who encouraged me to continue to pursue my writing and helped me throughout my writing process. I could have not made it this far without the support of so many!

First, I want to thank all those at Inscript Books who worked with me to prepare my book for publishing and all their support throughout the whole process. Giving me a chance in my writing means more than you know.

Thank you, Mom and Dad for always encouraging me and supporting me throughout my whole life. I never would have made it this far without y'all. Specifically, thank you Dad for teaching me everything about football and all the times we played backyard (which was actually in the front yard) football that inspired me to add football into the story. Thank you Mom for teaching me how to make my way around the kitchen and all the times that we had a blast baking and cooking. Y'all are the inspiration to Lacy's parents in the story. Thank you from the bottom of my heart for everything you have done for me. Love y'all so much!

To my siblings, who support my passion for writing and gave me inspiration for some of the characters in the story, regardless if they are aware of it or not.

To Hannah, one of my closest friends, who helped immensely and sacrificed her own time to help edit my drafts. Thank you for supporting me and always being there for me.

Annemarie, thank you for your friendship and being a constant cheerleader, encouraging me to fulfill my dreams.

Thank you to my new friend, tennis buddy, Spring Ma, for being my soundboard for writing my acknowledgments and bio.

Thank you, to all my friends and loved ones who have encouraged me throughout my writing process and celebrate this accomplishment with me.

To that special someone (you know who you are), I wrote this book before meeting you, but thank you for teaching me how to love someone again.

All my fellow readers and Instagram followers, thank you for following me on my journey to become an author and giving me a chance. Y'all are awesome!!

Most importantly- thank you, Lord, for giving me the desire to write and always giving me story ideas. Thank you for bringing me joy in writing and helping me persevere through the countless times of doubt that this day would ever come. Thank you for teaching me perseverance and coming to you for everything because you are the only one who can satisfy me.

Finally, to all those who have made the ultimate sacrifice for this country and their family members—I cannot express my gratitude for each and every one of you and for those who lost their lives to protect this country. Thank you is not enough.